Stomping the Goyim

D1604373

Michael Disend

Stomping the Goyim

MASTERWORKS OF FICTION
(1969)

GREEN INTEGER
KØBENHAVEN & LOS ANGELES
2002

GREEN INTEGER
Edited by Per Bregne
København/Los Angeles

Distributed in the United States by Consortium Book
Sales and Distribution, 1045 Westgate Drive, Suite 90
Saint Paul, Minnesota 55114-1065

(323) 857-1115 / http://www.greeninteger.com

First Green Integer edition 2002
©1969, 2002 by Michael Disend
Published originally in a slightly different version as
Stomping the Goyim (New York: Croton Press, 1969)
Reprinted by agreement with the author

"COOL JERK" (Copyright ©1966 McLaughlin
Publishing Co.) Lyric used by permission of
McLaughlin Publishing Co. c/o Mietus Copyright Management,
New York, New York.

This book was published in collaboration with
The Contemporary Arts Educational Project, Inc.,
a non-profit corporation, through a matching grant from the
National Endowment for the Arts, a federal agency.

NATIONAL
ENDOWMENT
FOR THE
ARTS

Design: Per Bregne
Typography & Cover: Trudy Fisher
Photograph: Michael Disend by Seymour Jacobs

LIBRARY OF CONGRESS CATALOGING IN PUBLICATION DATA
Disend, Michael [1945]
Stomping the Goyim
ISBN: 1-931243-10-7
p. cm — Green Integer: 56
I. Title II. Series

Green Integer Books are published for Douglas Messerli
Printed in the United States of America on acid-free paper.

To my parents

Contents

"Basically, every man's daughter is Jewish. If not, at least his aunt, green-grocer, musician, or bad self. Then what is a *goy*? Do such entities exist?"

The Breather

Post-Peace baby boom Spoddy.
Snarling, his body grew in Little Newark.
Snarling, he stomped the goyim.
And got cloudy, shriveled arm, a quitter.

Jews and gents, black or white, the old mystics whispered: "So tall, but a vile mouth." Twenty years old, he migrated to a tenacious New York basket inhabited by wretched Puerto Ricans, desperadoes, and habitués of chemical constellations. He brewed these grieving chemicals. He sold these chemicals to eat. His violent health increased to the flutter of real-world rampage. He learned to guffaw at knife-point. The front door of the crumbling hole called Evil Companion: the back door slammed like the Sorry Kid. The virus resembled a hobo two hundred years ago. Then the coldest society in recorded history resurrected amnesia in Asia and Spoddy felt the military's ancient snores.

And ducked.

This is common in Amur'ka.

1 / Egg Cream Boy Stumbles

For draft advice, I consulted

Evil Companion —
METHODS ARE EYE-BALL BUSTING. DONE WITH THE FIRST
AND SECOND FINGERS OUT LIKE PRONGS, CONSCRIPTION
IS AVOIDED. AFTER ALL, MOST PEOPLE REFUSE TO
ACKNOWLEDGE THE EXISTENCE OF THESE PERVERTS
UNLESS YOU DANGLE IT SHORTENED. HIRE A SHOEDOG,
PRINT LEGIBLY

and Ira's comical head, a roseate bas-
ketball, told me how to make a DMT movie. He had
this faucet-nosed cold. Eyes itch, glands trot for the
night, popping sanitation.

Worried about Barbie, I warned him: "If you like
your blue candy of a cock, stop blackmailing me.
Describe the movie."

He dribbled ashes on his crotch. A twenty-six year
old psychology grad, his voice isn't inside him any-
more. Wooden buttons, rope loops on his suburban coat.
It blended nicely with wide-wale corduroy pants.

"Sure, OK. Open with pan shots of the crowd. Set
cameras from four directions. They'll go in and out,
back and forth. The crowd's the same crowd that's in

the theatre then. Get it? There's a film of a movie and then it pulls back as it shows the audience, but from three sides. The same crowd that's in the theater is on the screen of their screen. Get the old ladies, the groping couples, the queers in the last row, the evening children. Focus their faces close up. You get the plush of the seats. Then you spasm, shimmer, and still . . . ."

"You do what again?" Was the last of the ready-made mind. "And roll a foot-long joint please."

Ira's specialty is extravagant length. Over his door hangs a plaque with this inscription: THE ROAD OF EX-CESS LEADS TO THE PALACE OF WISDOM

* billy blake.
He sneezed into an orange, polka-dot ascot and stepped on his memory. Why? Drugs ruin your memory. Drugs give you the chills. Drugs make you silly. Spoddy's known and disobeyed that dictum half his choosy life. But simple folk don't hunger the doctorate for six years.

"It's simple with the right equipment, as the old adage. You just spasm, shimmer, and still. Dig it? Then the camera falls on a gentlewomanly couple. She says to her maiden sister ACHHANU HOLLAGADOO. The maiden sister turns to the accountant on her left. She says to him ACHHANU HOLLAGADOO. He repeats softly to the sailor ACHHANU HOLLAGADOO. The whole row is saying ACHHANU HOLLAGADOO. It attacks the street, the city itself. The whole state is trumpeting ACHHANU

HOLLAGADOO! Then you fade to a shot of these our United States. You make it spasm, shimmer, and still. You pull the camera back until you have the earth in your lens, throbbing like it's got blue-ball. The DMT-drenched universe is crying ACHHANU HOLLAGADOO!!!"

Ira is technically inadequate. Interns kiss the symptoms, not the man. I tested my pyramids while he rolled and riffed. Took the dictaphone mouthpiece and let the Sorry Kid whimper:

> *'Listen, man, Skip a lot away.*
> *Mother's prowling. She tells*
> *Your Family Doctor Cole*
> *about the Boys next door, the*
> *Stories told to Amuse a*
> *select Klatch. He hesitates*
> *to Checkmate the Parent's*
> *Right to a Money-made life.*
> *He drinks Mommy's iced-tea*
> *that August afternoon,*
> *Prescribed Pills for the*
> *Ailment.*
> *(His Divided Self remedies*
> *were Western hangovers,*
> *man)*
> *Mommy scents Indiscretion*
> *and Sprinkles arsenic on the*
> *Cucumber Slices.*

Cucumber Slices are Soggy in
Salad Dressing in the lazy
susan. At which Point he
don't Eat no Salads she
Make for the Ice-Cream Box.
He Nails Mommy.

I'm Adept — mon cher — at
Air Polkas.'

Before I can register the Kid's oracle, Ira's back with a cigar-plump joint. Glancing at the mouthpiece in my hand: "Still focking with psychotic playthings Spoddy? You know, your house smells like curry all the time." A chef, friends boast of special services when cashless. Ieeyow! they squeal, he done a miracle with three eggs and a mouldy pumpernickel crust. I believe in rice-absent miracles, so I requested:

"Browneyes, it's been weeks since you've been by. Why not the honor of making dinner for me, yourself, and Mr. Funny? He'll be home soon. The refrigerator's yours."

Peevish, he turned wooden and teased Sundown Magic Alice. Spoddy's kitty sleeps in a basket suspended from the living room ceiling. Living room, kitchen, two bedrooms = my grassy house. She pressured Ira's thigh, free cat in heat that day. He passed the giant joint to me, and while I dragged: "There's this, Spoddy. Mr.

Funny's perversions make me queasy. Irrational, but I can't dine comfortably with a guy in a dress."

Jive. How is it, I thought, that with all your cold-cream parties, your jewels in the navel, hashish serenades, eclectic cinema, you can't tolerate his lace? But I was saved a hassle when Mr. Funny burst in. Ira blushed, so my roommate collapsed in his lap. Tender explosion.

"Not now sweet stuff," said Ira, pushing him off and crossing his cuffless corduroy legs, "I've got my own." He took a root from his pocket and, ignoring Mr. Funny, stuck it under my nose. "Sniff that and understand how half the world lives."

Did. "What is it?"

"Ginger. Touch it lightly with your tongue . . . ."

A ghost who's slept with generals won't be denied. Frisked me expertly when I'm half asleep. Sometimes allow it: sometimes don't. My ephemeral roommate shrilled in: "Want to know what I learned today? I learned from that lovely Breather that to make a peacock spread its lovely, multicolored tail, you address the bird politely 'Finark, Finark.' Isn't that marvelous? Finark! Finark!" He danced among the benches, hammock, and chairs: "Finark! Finark! Finark!"

Nothing bloomed but Ira's indignation, sulking to the kitchen. Spoddy watched Mr. Funny gyrate and heard eggs break. Butter sizzles and a goody-good smell. As my roommate sauntered the odor to its source, I joined them, ready to play mediator. Mr. Funny measured Ira's ass. He turned to me, palms apart, thumbs touching. "Spacious." The kingpin of graduate vice did an about-face.

"Look, have I ever done anything to offend you?" He's excellent, pouting. Recall him telling me he wouldn't burn the bird, if snared, unless the narcos notified grandmama, a vital yin source in the fellowshipless days ahead. An ingratiating soul.

Mr. Funny scurried to his bedroom, back in a moment. Spread arms languid from body and twirled stylish pirouettes.

"What's it called?" gasped Ira, trying to maintain.

"A body stocking. And this is a half-slip. It sort of slips away." Sundown Magic Alice sniffed his ballet slippers, pounced on his lap. Mr. Funny nestled the kitty to his green nylon groin and stroked it. "Feels so good when she moves around." Handing me a manila envelope. "Do you like these latest creations?"

Spoddy thumbed thru the series of sketches and found the familiar curly-haired heroes in lingerie. Fashion artist was the roommate's uneven income. But he shouldn't have used my face.

"Ain't no prude, only don't peddle these hereabouts." Neon kitchen lights were replaced by dinnertime candles.

8

"Don't sweat it," said he, nibbling Ira's diced red peppers. "I'm just trying to convince you that you'll look *it* in silks. Being a phallic woman has extra-military advantages if you're in love with textures. Once a child," he orated, "my sister poured milk in the guts of her dolls. And despite the necessity of folding these eternally silent children at the middles in order to belch a 'Mama, Mama, Mama' from their tin egos, she knew. Compensated with her unlearned . . . uh . . . maternity. Like me."

Ira set a platter of steaming eggs flecked with chips of beef and peppers between us. Yellow, red, brown. Curtsied and said: "This one's name is Ira's Balls-Up-Boost," ladling a petite portion to Mr. Funny upon whom he cast opprobrium-filled looks. Icepick looks, as it were, so to speak.

"I was talking about my dear sister. Shown you those photos of her, haven't I Spoddy? It means I'm fixated. Ira, you've got the face of a friendly pony. National Velvet cutey-pie."

"ACHHANU HOLLAGADOO," murmured Ira, winking at a deadpan me. Tucked white napkin at his throat.

Excitement flushed Mr. Funny's creamy face. Licking his lips: "O, I've heard of that. You chew ice and then suck off. Also called the High Hum." Tipped his glass of Leapfrog Milk over, and a trickle stained his half-slip. He pulled it around so the wetness clung his thighs.

"I've got to split," announced Ira. "Your roommate is badtripping me. This freak is tolerable another time, but not after I've cooked. Not if I'm noshing either." Eggs getting cold, and he hadn't removed his coat. Mr. Funny, from the tail of my eye, was reaching for the chutney. Casual cripple. Fluid. Some people are like depth bombs. I never pity them.

"Hey Ira," hissed Mr. Funny, "before you leave us, I want to explain myself to you." Water dripped in the sink. Blue candle made us sinister. Electric bass exotics quarreling on quarter-note time. Mine is a musical house. "Here's a ballcutter for you. When I was in military school the penalty for smiling on drill formation was hike your skirts and gallop in full dress uniform around the assembled cadets for three miles . . . ." His eyebrows arched violet, jaw grinding like astrologers on leave. "You hadda chase your smile. I repeat, baby, you had to *chase your hernia smile*!!!" Adjusting his underthings, lady aroused wrongly. "Does that explain me proper?"

"A fact my six years of graduate study done taught me," said Ira, pissing in the sink, voice sounding doubly disembodied in the dark, "is that pharmacists aren't familiar with herbs beyond their natural context." Kissed my roommate's hand, departed like a hashish wisp where the fatboys assemble.

Mr. Funny washed the dishes as I submitted to

10

Evil

Companion — PAINT YOUR BALLS BLUE. THE MEDIC WILL
PLOTZ AND THINK IT A VARIANT OF CROTCH ROT. SYMBOL
OF DECAY. TELL HIM IT LAUNDERS BUT YOU LIKE IT BLUE
EVERY WEDNESDAY. A METHOD WORKING WONDERS IN
LITTLE NEWARK

and imagined the splicing on Ira's film.
(Needed: a quart of DMT and a quiverful of African Black
gage) I sipped Leapfrog Milk as glistener to my pre-induction physical. It's a drink of Spoddy's invention, a tangy
genii dispensing three wishes when I reach maturity.
Around the dawn's early light I began reciting Sorry Kid
proposals, entertained by the appropriate metanoia. Mr.
Funny had fixed me a scrambled yin snack before bed-
ding down to dreams of the Joint Chiefs of Staff renting
him to crawl across the floor hissing PZZZZZ-PZZZZZ
sounds while wrapped in cobra skin. Spoddy felt fine,
unafraid of the ensuing State machinery.

5 A.M. came this frightful rapping at my door.
Barbie.

"Your calm isn't my calm!" she shouted. O hush, I
indicated with hand signals, and don't awaken Mr.
Funny who's wearing your overnight negligee for drag.
"Spoddy, you can chew off that tongue of fire for shit.
Tomorrow, I mean later, I'll learn whether I go war
widow, you shipped off to the Green Hell, and I'm not
supposed to yell? Is that fair? Is it?" The 'Big Is' rou-

tine. So noisy I wanted to put the boots to her. Yes, put the boots to the chick who sensed my hard body might never pass for an angelina's.

Ushered her to the bedroom.

"By the way I'm tripping. Blown down to zero. You pushed me into it." Fragrant airplane, Spoddy thought, wherein she'd soar discordantly for hours. She gasped at my plywood city miniatures thru a magnifying glass. Brushed a cheek to black/ smooth/ oily hair: she pulled away. "And I'll permit no brutality now. This body wasn't meant . . . ." Flinging Sundown Magic Alice cat off the bed and sprawled. Nostrils twitch. Mumbly pegs curled under her round. Her milky limbs huddled together. Television, Germany, dope: the agonies weren't slight. Spoddy had found her in the park. We'd been muff diving ever since. Lacerated my knees crawling for the drip drip drip.

"Barbie, you come here so wasted, so frantic. Draining your head that way won't do." Welcomed her, this Amur'kn high-school escapist, the way she'd consummated an eatable lay with the Dragon on St. George. 16 year old veteran of the psychedelic cornucopia, she tumbled yawning thru the private girls' school junk scene, the Central Park West analysis, the scraped uterus.

Yet Evil Companion wouldn't welcome her. He sneered, showed angry fangs. Probably reluctant because of her affection for the Ever-lasting Staircase, of which each step is eight inches high. It was Barbie, pretty Barbie, tattooed phoenix at 15, who taught me: "Where does the fire escape up it? Got a ready answer? Fuck no! Hell, Spoddy, is where the fire escape spirals." That modern misconception had to perish. It signified a secret faith in couch purification.

"Gangster of love," she said. "But I'm a girl and our *relationship* is on the verge. Seconds to go. Each time I — we — do the dirty deed it gets blacker. Back home I need oxygen. Also, you're swallowing me. Why?"

Hesitated. Said: "Anybody who loves me loves an Evil Companion."

She paced restlessly thru the room. Her gait, the denim miniskirt, were enough for loin incantation. Typical acidhead move, she froze before my series of Klee paintings. Staring at his AN INSIGNIFICANT FELLOW BUT OUT OF THE ORDINARY, said, "Christ, it goes in five directions in a sneaky way," chewing her thumbnail. I condescended closer while his thinking orbs sizzled her. Am I a tender man? Am I a feeble man? A hijacking finger below the panties left her icy. Fresh lettuce on pastrami smell curdled me. I gravitated to the dictaphone and the Sorry Kid correspondence.

"You're a stone motherfucker, Spoddy, a motherfucker."

Never did. Barbie's current illusion was of my pre-

13

natal plot innocence. The entrapment yen. Unnecessary. I was irritated. In two earth hours, on the State's time, was to be physicaled. What better way of waiting than to hustle the perimeter of Spoddy's fear to the hub, a demand equation task of utter concentration. Now a darling, primed to the ears, had me jumpy

Evil Companion — YOUR VIBRATIONS FADE. AN EARTH BATH IN ASIA IS AT STAKE. BEWARE THE HOSTESSES' BRILLIANT UNIFORMS

"... an insight for you," I said, mentioning her Tompkins Square sister. "The changes in Julia are staggering. After skimming thru the tunnel of dreck with Evil Companion, she can sleep alone. No more trips to the midnight salami. It surprised the crap out of me. I mean, she was his first cup of coffee, his last cup of tea. Let's toast them with Leapfrog Milk. Aloneness is soft, OK?"

She ran home wailing.

Troublesome house guests are the least of my worries. The first time the Sorry Kid cornered my throat I dispensed home-rolled fear and bought passivity. Guessed his only goal is health and let the man-of-wool have his say. Schizophrenia doesn't inspire Spoddy. But it's vital to stifle certain tendencies for fear of outraging Evil Companion whose wrath consists of

IT'S A

MEAN OLD WORLD. TRY LIVING IN IT BY YOURSELF. GO
ON: TRY IT — Evil Companion

                                    and energy fields.
Barbed, enclosed, energy fields. Call his punishment
the Easy Box, after riffs monastic. Two monks put a
third heretic in a wooden balls-high container, then
watch the character sweat a sinful past under a broiling
noon. And what upheaval would be worth my guardian's
loss? Certainly not the whinings of his bluebelly, the
Sorry Kid, an instigator of bloody canards. But,
Amur'kn democratic in origin, I examine each auricu-
lar telegram.

Nursing a tumbler of Leapfrog Milk, flipped a switch
and traced his diction:

> 'Listen, man, I met this Sophomore
> named Asatrucker who at some Point
> in a Rather Brief Conversation
> told me the Following Anecdote
> which I'm on the Point of Relating
> to You. It seems his Roommate
> in his Freshman Year was a Psychotic
> of Sorts, and he decided to Quite
> Deliberately Dominate Asatrucker
> through the Agency of a Radio.
> He would come into the Room Every
> Night at Three O'Clock in the
> Morning, Shine a Light in Asatrucker's

15

Eyes, Shit on the Floor, Shout a
Little, until Asatrucker Turned
On the Radio, at which Point
he would Cease all of this and Go
to Sleep. A Macabre Ritual,
no?
(SO'S THE GREAT SHOEDOG OF THE
NORTHERN SKY)
His Sinister Plan was to Condition
Asatrucker into Complete and Total
Dependence on the Radio, and then
One Day he'd Smash It. Asatrucker,
a stalwart youth, Saw Through this
Diabolical Scheme, and One Night
simply Paid No Attention. The
Antagonist's Destruction was Final
when Asatrucker won a Prizefight Bet
which Yielded $100 on a $100 Investment.
The Roommate Gave Up Everything and
from then on Slept Out in the Hall.
He was, in addition, Kicked Out of
School, when Two Fellows tried to
Keep him from Messing Around Too Much
and he Responded by attempting to
KILL Both of Them with a Machete.
(What would you think if the
Kid tried that?)

The Aftermath was Bold.
Thought, man, I could Fruitfully
Graft Some of You onto Me.'

The Sorry Kid has more dinero than you can shake a stick at. He don't need no government mediator. His U.S.A. oracle a classic example. The fool won't learn that a pathetic use of misnomers just start me wincing. Lariats of innuendo won't bag the Evil Companion: too broad in the shoulders. More disturbing, though, was the Kid's shrunken oral pride. He used to pimp his prophecies. Starched, ready-to-wear, elegant doodabs. To sleep in a dead man's shirt was beneath him. And now that *Radio* thing, that electronic slander!

Because I never identify with inanimate objects.

Because I never identify with inanimate objects.

17

2 / A Juicehead's Proposal

"What were some of the funny things said last night?"

"There were none."

I dreamt Barbie double in the hours before my draft physical. The Leapfrog Milk made me cotton-tongued and wretched. I dreamt:

"Is them some of our brethren?"

"Just niggers. Drive on."

        . . . about Barbie. Three months gone with that girl, a walking eye-feast. She blinks her lids like a Little Newark teacher trying to learn a pickaninny how to read in Hawthorne Avenue School where the black militants pinch her tits by the bus-stop. Flashcard method: "Now Louise, tell Miss Golden what 'mystic' means. Come on honey, you remember." — "Uh, uh . . . ?" (off to the side, wishing it were Yiddish) ". . . pig-tail headed nincompoop." Later, Miss Gold meets foaming Mr. Gangi the gym teacher in the lunch room. And over tea and Swiss cheese: "Did you hear what that big black Lawson boy did in music class? He was intercoursing with Belinda Bear and Mr. Muscatello told him to take his sneakybrim off in class and the animal said 'No fool stop mah ball' or something Spanish, and bashed the old man's lower plate down his throat. Then of course he took a razor and carved WHITEE SUCK PLUNGER on his forehead. The kids heard me twist and shout," her blank lemony face shook sadly. "If it weren't for the cops in the playground . . . ." She dreaded waiting for the bus at 3:30. The jitterbugs in front the pool hall got her well, you know, kinda uneasy . . . . Spoddy dreamt an apple-eyed Barbie doubletime. Once I walked with her on pastures and rivers and mountains and found another Barbie curled on a hill side. She asked: "Is the universe *really* a child playing with dice?"

It was Mr. Funny who woke me.

"Cause of crime is tardiness, Spoddy. Hurry, get dressed, and foul up our fatherland."

So I slipped into costume and made for the Selective Service building.

Little Newark, New Jersey — rainbow piss in a bucket — is pronounced like a pig's grunt

Evil Companion — NORK! NORK! LIDDA NORK!! TRY TENDERNESS and the Wide Street building was filled with dumpdown children. Italian, Irish, and mainly brown kiddos. These wallowing/mingling boys gave a collective NU-NUNU!?! at my appearance. Unique physiognomies and dress are scary in this cesspool city. The poor try to set the night on fire.

Spoddy's fag swish horrored a cartoon sergeant.

Spoddy drew Buddhist mandalas on the intelligence test.

Spoddy played mad dog and nipped a boy in the butt.

Spoddy, drily: "Help me I've got the influenza.
Lick me I've got the rag on."

. . . and soon a blushing corporal shouted: "Number 15 follow me!" And this patriot who'd never even cut himself shit/shower/shaving led the way.

"Wait here. The Jew's going to test you for real."

I snapped. "Can I suck you baby? Can I suck your cock before the new morning . . . ?"

This pink man, this corporal, telegraphed a roundhouse right to my nose. I slouched and stopped his aggression with a swift knee to the bellows, a chop to the larynx, as in Central Ward Karate Boogaloo. Those dozen fingers go for me. Into the cubicle I race and brace the door.

"Please negotiate," roared a dozen sounds, rattling the doorknob.

"Fuck your Selves," was my Renunciation and Love.

Secret for the masses: gunbearers got the One-Track Arm. In a moment the commotion subsided and I turned to find yet another heir of Moses and Marx, heavy knish scrutinizing me from behind a desk. I curtsied for the removal of lipstick, food stains, fruit stains, grease, and gravy.

Lieutenant Pocoloo — Amur'kn Army psychiatrist, priest of the hourglass — withered me once over and remarked, "The sick are a terrible burden. The *truly* sick, I mean." He lit a cigarette in defiance of the NO SMOKING sticker on his forehead and progressed, "But the phonies, the crew of shits that mark off what you've marked off — *if* they're phoney — we've got names for. We've got so many names for what you've marked off it's incredible. Also," winking at me, "thirty years in the federal penitentiary a way South." He gave that two savage minutes to work. Then, evenly, he ground out his new smoke on a leather wristband and demanded, "When did it start? What started it, your temptation?" Drumming his fingers, snorting.

"Crackerjacks, and the next thing I was on my knees before the sailorboy on the package . . . ," and was stopped by Lieutenant Pocoloo's palm, traffic-cop style.

Emptying his ashtray into his desk, he pulled the deaf-and-dumb lurk, and trembled. "Crackerjacks," he muttered. "Crackerjack kids do that too?"

"Around the clock, and they're so *sticky*," stigmatizing Evil Companion.

The lieutenant thumbed thru my folder, meanwhile bursting saliva bubbles with his tongue. His procedure intrigued. He inflated saliva until the shell hung phosphorescent over his lower lips, opaque, soon to splatter: then a pink point would eject and — Zzap — the

21

sea rejoins the rock-pool.

"Mr. Spoddy, what do you think of the War?"

"Shift it to Guatemala. You're needed in Guatema-lan *Bese–Me–Bongo* Insurrection."

"Mr. Spoddy, why'd you tilt over the tray of urine samples and then splash a toy duck in it screaming life is a cheese sandwich?"

"Vanity and lust."

He grinned, said in confidential tone: "Really, there's nothing to fear . . ." not mentioning the $300 government graveyard contribution to the family of the Little Newark paratrooper who, as the black-bordered tele-gram read, "got it in the head." So Spoddy didn't wor-ship the lie.

"Well Mr. Spoddy, I think maybe you're playing a game, aren't you? But you *have* checked off that box, haven't you Mr. Spoddy? And you *did* steal the wallets of six other inductees and hide them in your basket. Well, suppose you tell me number one why you're dressed th-that way," nicotined forefinger indicating my chartreuse hip-slung bell-bottom slacks sporting fifteen inch cuffs with rhinestones arranged in the shape of THE SHOEDOG, then my balloon-sleeved velour death-dance-dewdropped paisley overshirt and, lastly, the iron cross swaying at my left ear, a fascist nicety. "Christ, it makes you look like a girl, for Crissakes. Number two, how long it's been since you've had relations with your fellow man."

". . . if you can call that a face," I added, clasping both hands under opposite armpits. "By that, of course, the face of War. You see, War means for me that bicycle chains are used for braces, and there's a perfume ration. Mr. Funny told me that. It's verified in the texts. These same-size clothes are his I borrowed. Mr. Funny's funny with money, if I may stoop to waggishness, which is sort of a bringdown these days, nothing excluded. Can I smoke?"

Jabbing a finger at his forehead Lieutenant Pocoloo shouted: "What you think I got this sign here for? You kids I interview think that on account *I* smoke, *you* smoke. Look," he paused, lips pursed, "you're freaky, but I like you," and extended his pack of cigarettes. It was stone-cold empty. "You're pretty fast to break the rules, aren't you boy? Well, that's what you get when you break the rules. A big fat zero." Laughing, he tilted his chair back, fingers splayed on the desk. The sheepish sound of processed inductees shuffling outside his office caught my attention. He said: "Go on with your history, I'm fascinated. If you're nervous, jerk off. Isn't that what your rampaging under-age cronies told you? To jerk off the shrink, I mean shrink the jerkoff?"

"Definitely not," wearied at his insinuation. "Evil

Companion kept feeding me advice. I listened, but I always listen to Evil Companion, as it were, so to speak."

"Evil companion?"

"Evil Companion kindergarten clenched fist."

Comprehension spread gaslight across the lieutenant's face. He marked something on a yellow pad and gazed at me. "This friend — is he Catholic? Is he vigorous in a sensual backlash? You said 'evil.' Is your family religious of what common denominator? It's all falling into a kind of latticework pattern. When was the last time you, shall we prey, 'browned it?' Simmer down son."

Whole business was making me hungry. Spoddy yarbles placidly, in monotone. "Bio-psychic equilibrium you call it. I have other definitions. The last time the Sorry Kid was the bowl, Evil Companion the reamer. Last time — peace enough for me, though not in the vernacular," huffing the song along, "and I rarely leave my house."

Red/Black Fuse House.

Red/Black Outlaw House.

Red/Black Cowboy House.

Sun kind enough to shine upon a USA Selective Service board window flashed a bright scar upon over under Lieutenant Pocoloo's bag flesh.

"Tendencies," remarked the soldier, "are popping out

24

all over." He played with a pencil, frowning. "The way I look at it, your friend — boll-weevil-evil — as you so aptly phrased — has seduced you repeatedly and you've picked up various mannerisms, sensibilities, et cetera from him and it's probable — I should say obvious — that your sexuality is no longer the uh the good one? heh heh heh." Went through my folder officiously and said, "Well, get set for a big fat depression to begin." His right hand smoothed out the NO SMOKING sticker, curling into an eyebrow, the left hoisted a branding iron.

PERMANENTLY REJECTED — PSYCHIATRIC followed by a penned-in 'paranoid-schizophrenic homosexual panic state' was my afternoon destiny. Lieutenant Pocoloo pressed his temples thoughtfully, staring at his words. He said in friendly tone: "You know like the hook in the letter G? Did you ever think of it heated whitehot like a frenchfry and yourself hooked on it? Or like the point — what if you stuck a Viet Cong rascal in the desert and pinned him under the O worldling votary and let wild ants crawl up his nostrils? Or you tie him face-first to a D smeared with radioactive mint jelly and it rots his face shit-colored . . . ? I mean, do you portray torture with letters?"

"Not lately, no sir," the crooked angle.

Raising his head, he asked: "If the mothers of Amur'ka some day accept your kind in the service, in what way do you feel your, erh, peculiar tyro terrorism could be utilized?"

"Asatrucker," I answered

Evil Companion — OB-
JECTION: KISS LIEUTENANT POCOLOO ON THE LIPS. GO ON:
KISS THE FLY TO DRIZZLY SUBLIMATION

". . . there's
something I'm ashamed to ask you."

He navigated from behind his desk and assumed a
criminal cloak. His eraser lips twitchy twitchy: his flat-
ware mind wanting: his khaki belly . . . .

"O Jesus," moaned Spoddy, blossoming outside-agi-
tator tears.

3 / The Strange Duet

The living room collage startled. Spoddy passed thru the benches, hammock, and chairs with, "Look, it's terrible late afternoon and I'm dreadful exhausted. Good day to you too, you rollicking clowns," and made for bed. But friends' hands cupped an elbow and led me to a stool. This stool was in the center of the living room of my grassy house, which I expected empty. I drooped there, balloon sleeves ruffled, jaded as a child.

"Spoddy is floral today," aimed at two fresh faces. This in explanation of colorful clothes. "Spoddy is floral today." And breaking into song:

> "Dat's all dere is,
> dey ain't no more.
> Goddam de rich
> an' save de po'."

A light touch is often endearing. During the conversational void I noticed the two strangers had ribbed jaw muscles, as if they gnawed poplars after the soup du jour. Ghastly. "Is there any music? I come back from puberty rites in Amur'ka and there's no music. Ira, some lyrical hatred jazz."

Walking to the painted-over windows, I pretended to scout beyond the shellac. I heard whispered from behind: "I'm so happy you're safe. I was looking forward to seeing you all day, 'cause ah really feel fer you, ah feel it comin' on now fer gawdsakes, an me jes' *talkin'* a yah 'bout it. Pardon me, ah gotta take a coupla seconds to flip off and relieve the strain on my 73-yars-old overhauls." With those words Mr. Funny's adroit fingers plucked the iron cross from my swollen lobe and I faced the alliance.

"Foolish neophytes," I said, "and fast friends. Please excuse my nastiness of a few moments ago, but consider the recent whereabouts." Bowed from the waist and forced a Sorry Kid smile. "They're having this grim combat and wanted me."

Hard-bop Chicago saxophones sounded on the victrola.

Arthur Ogle, coterie pal, bounced a tennis ball off the window sill, said: "The Spoddy is in session. This body is out of order. Did you make it? How'd it go?" The ball took a bad spin and landed in a newcomer's lap. He raised his upper lip like a curtain, a coquette's skirt, and showed brazen fangs. Stalagmite incisors, curved. Glowering like a ten-minute egg, he stuffed the ball into his pocket.

Arthur Ogle scratched his jugular. "That's terrifically unjust."

"I like to bite, only to bite . . . ," whispered the stranger, shy as the dickens, unlike

Evil Companion
— GIVE THE LOUT A TASTE. HE'S ALOOF, RIDDLED WITH SOUVENIRS AND CAVITIES

I stepped forward. "Mister, you're in my house. My house welcomes ne'er-do-wells, only I have to be introduced. And there's these rules to follow." As Lieutenant Pocoloo's reprimand echoed me, I screamed: "Cruelty is so all over that the 20th century persists by default. Our generation — I'm loyal to it — has come and gone. My house is on the tundra, on the steppes, my seedless house is a play-room when everybody's forgotten how." Scooping Sundown Magic Alice from her basket, I whipped the yowling kitty at him. "I moved out of the country and bought this house. But there's a landlord. Don't ask me why. I thought I owned my time and a government showed. They don't mind the sun cancelled, just leave the trap-door alone. And remember," dropping the cat on his head, "him and me are the power twins."

The toothy fellow did the arrogant toss and Sundown Magic Alice landed feet first, as cats do. He straightened, flashing gums, vivid, alarmed. His look-alike buddy did the same. Then good-timing Mr. Funny loomed in, giggling. "Spoddy, Spoddy, Spoddy — forgive me. I have the piles and wasn't thinking. These two boys I met in the park, like you did Barbie," that allusion a soul needle, "and they're fine. Let me introduce you to the Bihder brothers."

Hands shaken: Ira, Natasha, Liz the localized troll, Mr. Funny, and Arthur Ogle got his ball returned unpunctured by the Bihder brother.

"That's a tripping mouth you got," said Ira. "You both got such grinders?"

The brothers squirmed together. "We like to bite, only to bite." It was hard differentiating the pair, and I reached for Ira's goat-skin cigarette case, exhumed a joint, moistened it. Hugged the smoke and watched Ira press.

"I'm courteous, but don't you people sleep? You can't bite all day and not sleep. It makes for fusion fission fascism. Explain yourselves."

The brothers probed each other's eyes. Ages of forest communicated. "We're Bihders," said the one who'd copped the ball. "My name is Joseph and baby's name is Franz. Joseph and Franz Bihder. If you can't tell us apart, look at our chins." Our cozy group investigated the two. Joseph's chin sprouted a purplish moss, while his brother's resembled the glazed flesh of the American Indian. "Our chins metamorphose after we go a-biting. It's purely chemical. Biting is not. Biting is rarified. You see, we like to bite."

SPAWNED A CONSTANT

30

HEADACHE — Evil Companion

                            thru fear, things came to a pretty pass

                 Evil Companion — RIDE IN THE EASY BOX PAST THE HONEYMOON STAGE

                           "You're making me nervous," warned Natasha, rolling a newspaper into a literal club.

Franz Bihder's gnarled fingers kept clawing down his thigh: his tusks were evident. Insisting: "Hi hi hi hi, I'm th-, the, I'm the, the Bihder. Hi! I meant, I'm the, the Bihder and I like to, to — to bite, only to bite. I like to, to bite . . . ," he tip-toed across the room, weaving among benches hammocks and chairs, hands hooked like gardening utensils. Confronting Natasha's closed thighs, booted knees, he dropped to his own. "Hello, I like to bite, only — only to bite, biting, to bite, bite, I'm the Bihder, only to bite, to bite . . . ."

Achievement of silence while his ivories shredded her boots was Natasha's triumph. Contrasting Barbie, her shrieks vanish under duress. The girl's cheeks bloomed as he spit leather chunks. She even bobbed her tits fondly to his shoulders when he had trouble with the inch-high heels. While he shlurped her ankle, we smoked.

"He's ravished," said Joseph, watching his brother, "to bite, only to bite the president's neck."

Mr. Funny wore sandals whose straps bound his legs like a trellis. Bad omen. And he shuddered voluptuously as Franz' well-worked tools honed on. I anticipated his variation of orgasm and the jealous, "Very sophisticated fags imitate women almost as well as Natasha can."

"Militarism in Amur'ka must be ruined." Yellow Afghanistan hashish was contributed by Liz the localized troll, and gainfully exploited. "So bite those boots! Munch those boots! Chew those boots!"

Evil Companion's malice flung shadow nets over my cries. I was again the Easy Box as cold-war relic. Paranoid Spoddy rode innumerable elevators to be repaved in the dark. I trundled to the kitchen and snatched a bag of potatoes.

"The Swinebowl Game!"

I tossed a potato to Arthur Ogle, another to Joseph Bihder, left 1-2-3 to Ira, ricocheted off the breasts of Liz the localized troll, wrapped Natasha's foot in the burlap sack, flipped a staple to Franz, again to Ira, reversed to Arthur Ogle, aloof to Mr. Funny, spit-potato to Joseph, back to Natasha, under the table to Franz and on and on and on and on and on until we puffed heated brains.

Ingrown walls are the Easy Box. Literally an absence of menagerie appeal. If the squeeze gets rough, I nourish on the Swineball Game, hoping to grow big muscles to cease implosion. Friends get victimized and dejected:

it's unpleasant watching Spoddy brace between the small of his back and dirty toes. There we were, evening chimes a-tingling, all about my house. The room was sagging. Exhausted.

Franz polished his fangs with a chamois strip.

Natasha stuffed Sundown Magic Alice down her unscarred boot.

Ira said of the southeast Asian toy, "So light 'er up, light the fucking pipe already, light 'er up."

Liz the localized troll informed us: "To refurbish a woman, they shove a ham-hock up the spout and pull out the bone."

And puppy-pooped Mr. Funny rested his head on my lap, the clotheshorse retroactive. I soothed his shoulders by thumb. He chewed that thumb and sat up.

"Spoddy, handicapped veterans like me have had to learn to think positively. You should know," he said, withdrawing a letter from his bosom, "that Barbie was by this afternoon. No comment on your vice, but she's a loon. She gave this for you and whistled some Yusef Lafeef melodies, an impossible chore. Spoddy, your girl is a loon." Very prim, he resettled his coiffure on my knees.

The letter was crayoned like a rainbow, adorned with schizophrenic mandalas. It read: IT'S NOT THE LSD DOING ME IN. IT'S THE SUGAR CUBES BLASTING MY COMPLEXION. PLEASE FIND ME — love, Barbie.

Crumpling the letter, I allotted two minutes for sorrow. Then, sucking quickly on the hash pipe, I nodded to Franz Bihder, said: "Your jaws work for a plywood city?"

His bestiality was guarded. ". . . I like to bite."

Smoky haze and the great compression of the Easy Box made my stroll to the exhibit loopy. Friends streamed ahead to the bedroom, turned on the lights. When Evil Companion arranges it so I can neither stand, squat, nor lie down, the needed remedies are divorced of apology. His torture is astute, unique. Even where jellied gasoline drenches the tongues of entire provinces, our occupying troops neglect the manufacture of Easy Boxes.

"Eye this," I said, pointing to a metropolis in microcosm, entirely carved from plywood chunks. "Note the lawns of green felt, the baroque firehouses, the priest walking his three-legged dog. Observe curved streets, following the French pattern before the revolution. Barricades were still possible. I got churches and brothels and insurance companies and playgrounds painted orange with toothpick jungle gyms like that indefinitely." Excluding the Bihder brothers, my allies were familiar with this paradigm of my devotion to city-planning.

"What's it for?" asked Joseph Bihder, licking his festooned lips, blessed by the asteroids.

" 'What's it for?' " I laughed, pretzeled in delight. "Why, man, it's for *you!*" And hoisting a tiny street-sign in the air, I cried: "Pick any unnamed avenue, any unnamed house, alley, garage, gas station, or even an army reserve shower-room. Go on. Name it and it's yours."

First suspicious, the brothers then receded the wicked dentures and probed Spoddyville eagerly. While they hunted down a home, the rest of the misfits sprinkled orange-gooey DMT on hash and wondered why their minds went bloodless. Inhaled the screaming Popes, the poison warp, excepting

Evil Companion — YOU TAKE THE LEAD IN THE TROUGH AND THEN WONDER THE INCHING INCHING INCHING EASY BOX, THE DIMINUENDO OF HUGS

and myself, who was suddenly furious. How much pressure can a man stand? Barbie's letter sliced paper cuts in my palm. Separating Spoddy from his exotic peers is a penchant for authoritarian bloodbath.

"Find a home to live in!" I hollered at the brothers, letting my right flank elude me.

They looked at me, stunned, and hastily combed the topography. They had the refugee jitters. Franz Bihder fingered a brown-white mansion, set near a tiny orchard, "This one, this one, to *bite* . . . ."

"I'm sorry, kids, but that's Ogle Castle."

Joseph Bihder peered at a cottage thatched with Barbie's black hair, situated beneath a bridge. Its span had taken straightpins and beaming hours.

"Please, it won't do. Liz the localized troll sleeps under that arch. She rents to foreign whirligigs."

It was a booby-trapped blowjob, the State all over again. Yet the brothers, informed of urban renewal problems, kept selecting sites. The tone of the skit grew fraught with despair and beefy, undulating anguish.

"This garage, this garage, bite bite bite . . . ."

"Unfortunately," I replied, "the city condemned it."

"To bite that meadow, the meadow!"

"Sorry, the poppy harvest next week."

At last popped the trap of reluctant interrogatives. The Bihder brothers wanted it expurgated. Regarding me with new impatience, Joseph Bihder whinnied: "If you aren't more careful, you go quicker to the grave, bitten. We like to bite."

Liz — localized troll halfslipped — was waltzing with Mr. Funny in the hallway, lagging, the blue-red underwater DMT rushing arteries. I called to them. "My call, my call . . . ." Wrapping my arms around Liz's concave body, placing her before me, I reacted to Joseph's slander. "Haven't you heard? We don't blockbust Spoddyville to Bihders." And a smile dietetic climbed my ears.

They prepared the attack by spacing out and growling the tinhorn: "Bite, we like to, to bite, only to bite, biting, to, to, to bite . . . ."

Liz the localized troll did well: hooded her face and wept until, led by an irate, ring-tailed Arthur Ogle, my congregation reeled in from the living room. And they stood there, staring, captivated by Liz's dyke haircut, the tears. More — they gazed quivering, they leered blasphemously. A character delineation occurred. A paralysis in cotton panties. As the Bihders knew the menace of the Spoddy circle, we saw their teeth melt in the thrashing energy of dope. Somebody struck a match. Rasp of sulphur. Mr. Funny, ever loyal, draped a variety of cotton baby-dolls 'n rompers, shifts, and button gowns soaked in chloroform and DMT over their heads. Ira had his amateur camera going.

Organized Bihder religion: a horde of women thrusting themselves upon the universal cock.

"I LIKE TO BITE!"

4 / Peek-a-Boo Artist

"Frankly, I don't know whether to shit or go blind," said Lieutenant Pocoloo. "There's a pain that extends from crotch to throat when I see you, you one-faggot pestilence."

"Sounds like the beginning of love."

He boomed his hand on the table. "When I had guys like you under me, in the Big Red One, a creep said to fart and cover an eye. But with you, Mr. Spoddy, that doesn't help. Look," and there was peanut-gas and the imitation of cyclops, "I swear it don't help."

Tugged my wand for comfort, said, "When you had guys like me *under* you?"

"No, by Jesus, not that way, you . . . you . . . ."

It was first inexplicable why the music of Benny and The Dirty Face blasted from the lieutenant's stereo, being so beyond his ken. Then, as the oblong patch of flesh where his NO SMOKING sticker had been sweated bullets and bullets, I got the knowledge: the soldier was a peek-a-boo artist. I loaded two ashtrays and awaited the dude's encroachment.

"You questioning why I called you to my apartment tonight, huh? Well, it's about a survey I'm taking for the board on ways to beat the draft. I mean, books been written on it, but I thought — surely — you'd expertise me on such matters close to your noodle. It'll also amuse you that I know you eluded me, maybe, on the firing line. Powdered curls and outfit don't fool me. When a man's got balls," staring fixedly at mine, "I know it. I know it, when a man's got balls or not."

Spoddy splashed his rum/coke on the floor, a minute glistener next to Leapfrog Milk, so's to mark wet coils with my toes. Pussywillowed my eyes and hummed: "Get yourself together. You know that isn't why you called me here, dear Pocoloo."

"Damn, it is," and he flung an envelope on the Chippendale coffee table between us. "Those pictures I think will interest you." The man poured himself a skyscraper whiskey.

I tore open the envelope, amazed to see Mr. Funny's sketches of Spoddy in mild garments.

"Where'd you get these?" I blurted.

"Ha ha ha!"

"Where'd you get these slanders?" I demanded, popping a sedative in my mouth. Cyclic calm is deafening.

Lieutenant Pocoloo licked the follicles on back of his hand, belched. "O, let's just call it a triangle cum business. Of the heavenly rank, that is."

"Alrighty," I drawled, lazybones incorporated, "you got the goods. What else?"

"More is needed?" He shuffled thru the pictures for a moment, then rolled up his sleeves. "I got the hairiest of wrists Spoddy, the hairiest of wrists. And where duty's concerned, these last few months have produced second thoughts. Is it true — ahahaha! — is it true that certain of your peers have been tying one leg behind their ass and rolling down the steps before breakfast?"

Spoddy pondered some pinwheel histories.

"Say it again."

Evil Companion — THE GREAT SHOEDOG OF THE NORTHERN SKY TAKES CARBOLIC DIPS, MEDICATED BATHS FOR THE NEW PRISONERS AS ANTI-LICE PROTECTION

and the rock 'n roll of Benny and The Dirty Face is after-dinner music for sweet young things of nine genders. In front of a docile calliope and inexperienced guitars Benny moans of life in the city. Now they laced into a little number called 'You've Got to Hate' and Lieutenant Pocoloo's chops gushed mellow: "Those dodgers tie a left leg behind a left thigh and roll — bumpetybumpbumpbump — down the stairs. Then they eat the cornflakes happy because they want to lose the use of the legs. The loss of the leg makes it impossible to serve." He bellowed it: "To *serve*, you hear? To serve us idiots!"

The lieutenant was built like a yesteryear barfighter, weight plumb in his ass. Ridiculous to knock about. If he was at a party, he'd dance one hand behind his back, the distilled hornpipe. I knew a character — Punch, from Little Newark — who if he didn't get his nightly bar brawl it was coitus interruptus. He'd come home and wake his wife — 'How bout a few rounds honey?' — and they'd don 22 ounce gloves and tap to sleep. Lieutenant Pocoloo was growling over me. "You hear? To serve the idiots, not to, they tie themselves behind the legs and fall." His behavior mirrored the laundry-man named Punch from Little Newark.

"A second now, as it were, so to speak. It's cotton-candy in my head. What does this riff mean?"

He gaped his maw in mine and whispered it phoneti-cally: "Listen, they their legs behind their back-wacky, do stroll dow' the stairees. The goddamn leg broke to not serve the gov for waree," dashing his whiskey in my face, "and not *serve* as they every able-bloodied good guy gotta!"

Snorting the drink from my nostrils, I said: "Back-ward Spoddy faces you. Give us a classical example."

He tottered to an electronic lamp, jerked it from its socket, whirled the fixture against the wall until the cord was loose. Handing it to me, he said, "Pay attention Spoddy. I'm going to hit the floor," — a noisy upheaval — "and now I'll get sexy, resemble a stiff-life." Fold-ing a leg under him, he panted, irrigating like a roast pig with an apple in its mouth, grunted: "Tie me leg

41

behind my leg. It hurt. Hurry."

Slick as sin, I tied a fancy bow. "OK?

Evil Companion — IMPROVISE A PANEL HOUSE AFFAIR

". . . or shall I tie the other one too?"

"Indeed, they fall and fall . . . ," said the lieutenant. And I trussed both his legs. Chicken delight in Amur'ka. Yoked. Only his forearms free, this army psychiatrist, this priest of the hourglass, dragged himself along the floor like a basketcase crab muttering, ". . . loose legs, can't ferve. War! . . . they can't, eating the cornfalls so sappy, phonies, phon . . . ," until he reached the apartment door.

I swung it open, bellboy resplendent.

"Watchit," said the lieutenant, and crawled to the edge of the steps. He hung his head over the top step and gazed down the black stairwell for the longest time. He gazed and gazed. There was a longer hum than the longest hum. He gazed and gazed. Finally, his chin flopped over the step edge and he snored.

Back in his apartment, I encountered the mirror, most perfect torture yet devised. I undressed and looked at Spoddy's legs, porcelain, white extensions, a rash of blonde fur Evil Companion —

ALMOST TONIGHT —

THE PANEL-GIRL IN THE PANEL-GAME. CLOSE THE OFFICE

FOR MONTH OF DRECK. MOVE TO SIMILARLY EQUIPPED
ESTABLISHMENT. YOUR BAG OF GREENBACKS

rapidly I
dressed, resentful of the sexual defamation. I can't leave
Barbie alone. I'm right back in the same old bag.

Lieutenant Pocoloo was still unconscious, chin over
the abrupt abyss. Preoccupied with SHOEDOGian
thoughts, I approached:

"Lieutenant? Sir . . . ?"

Withstanding no reply, I lifted his trousers behind
his stumped knees and flipped him down the stairs. He
rolled like a snowball. To quote: bumpetybumpbumpbump, and cartilage crushing echoes. Yet there was no
excuse to kick his nose to red paste, as in French Savaté.

5 / Declensions of Easy Box

Relative calm prevailed, despite the declensions of Easy
Box. I operated the dictaphone as a lark, stopped being
nearsighted about finances. That raging bullyboy, the
Sorry Kid, knows no hours. Few pundits do:

> *'The Roommate Returned, more*
> *Indigestible than Before. An*
> *Anecdote of Asatrucker's Plight*
> *will certainly Please You, for*
> *Disguised as the Most Well-Read*
> *Kid in the Colony, the Roommate*
> *took Asatrucker Hiking through*
> *Various, Secret, Unexplored*
> *Terrifying, Vast sections that*
> *Began and Ended*
> *off lockable doors*
> *off lockable windows*
> *& that had no Lights and Rickety*
> *Walls and Streams underfoot and*
> *Clinging to the Ceiling*
> *occasionally Dropping on Asatrucker's*
> *Squatty Head and Asatrucker was*
> *hysterically Terrified about being*

Eaten Alive by his Guide, whom
he'd only Known for a few days
anyhow, or his Guide suddenly
Metamorphosing into a Lachrymose
Bihder
       and

            leaving Asatrucker with
his Arms Ripped Off, unable to fend
away the Bihder Disciples
                    Chewing Out
his Corneas, Tearing into Asatrucker's
Cheek Flesh to the Skull, Nibbling
Asatrucker's Lips, Tunneling through
Asatrucker's inner Ear, Gnawing out
Asatrucker's Tongue . . . . . (If You
ever Drop in, I'll take you along)
Because of These Fears, Asatrucker
Desisted from his Lovely Odyssey
and went back to His Room to Wait
for the Consummation of his Planning
———— the Girlfriend's Call:
"Forget the concert. I've got dope,
baklava, and Irish Coffee here, and
seventeen million dollars willed
me by the late
            GREAT SHOEDOG
OF THE NORTHERN SKY,

who's my uncle,
and I love you insidiously. Fuck
me and I'll make you the happiest
and best paid man in the world."
But Asatrucker's Roommate Trilled
as she was Late by
ten minutes . . .
twenty minutes . . .
thirty minutes . . .
forty minutes . . .
fifty minutes . . .
sixty minutes . . .
To make a Long Story Short,
it was Mid-Lifetime and She
Still hadn't Called.
Can't trust a Nigger.
Asatrucker
one Hand Motionless on the Telephone
Waited in his Room.'

Hawking love, Barbie fell into my arms, "That peyote slop will steal the eyeballs out of your head."

Lapping my chin drool, Barbie mumbled, "I understood you at last when you stared at the ground, downcast, and asked Mr. Funny to fix you a peanut butter and jelly sandwich."

Barbie got spaced-out. "Astro-reality adore you baby?"

46

"Why do we use, why do we use, why do we use the drugs? Why do we use, why do we use, why do we use the drugs? Why do we use, why do we use, why do we use the drugs?"

She retreated to the hammock. Crisis, and Barbie goes prone. Peeling the tape from our dilemma she said: "Love rots when not stirred. There is a thing you feel with someone, so that you're no longer in conflict, in opposition to another human being. How rare! And what is worse — how delicate, how easily destroyed. No matter, Spoddy, how many years I live to see, I can't replace my dreams with my consciousness. Spoddy, dig onto me. I'm always a child . . ."

IS IT IN COLOR? ASK THE LADY IF IT'S IN COLOR. RAVE ON ABOUT NON-UNION CLERKS IN LITTLE NEWARK, MISLEAD — Evil Companion

but before I could agitate, she continued, ". . . and the very quality of the dream proves it. Listen to me Spoddy. You won't listen. Sometimes I'm like a stopped toilet . . . ."

Ended it inaccurate. "Shush! You're an inventory I took already. You're a known quantity. Down to the patterned hose and the part in the middle."

Pausing upsets me. If I can't wedge my nose between shards of snatch and play jungle, I sleep. Pausing for the intake, the re-entry, is a clogged affair. I built a teepee of fingers, perhaps to brood. She blinked her eyes: "OK then, we're over." Caressing her flaming bird tattoo, "I'll only scream so loud, spread my legs so wide."

That threat, and the bleak adjectives reveling within me, the comeuppance of Evil Companion's biggest hangup — thinging it — prompted me to lead Barbie to the bedroom. I lit an incense diamond. I unsheathed my boots. I let the black-velvet leggings drop. I unwrapped my chest from shirts.

Mounting was a deception.

"Don't you spell Narcissus with an N? Aren't you eating well? Meat makes you sluggish." A private moon in her rounded whites. "You made me promise not to trip here because of the policeman gambling next door. That's fair. But to come by after flashing at a thousand micrograms, after walking barefoot on gravel and feeling no pain for this disappointment . . . ," sighing.

What retorts for the allegations of the Sorry Kid? Between metaphors and a bleak Christmas in Vietnam, petrification was accomplished. Was Barbie, after all, kin to the GREAT SHOEDOG OF THE NORTHERN SKY? Will it wilt in the Easy Box? I pleaded with a girl, whispering: "Barbie, Barbie, all of your skin is like the inside of your thigh. You're sixteen. Don't evaporate on me."

Evil Companion — YOU COPPED OUT ON LITTLE NEWARK. FLUNKED. BE OUTRAGED BY DAYLIGHT SAVINGS TIME

48

my throat was parched. Flaky terror of nuns revived. Staphylococcus germs condemned the milk-machine muscle. Spoddy wore a tie to dodge the strep-throat and outlaw cigarettes in the ward. These mutual consolations particled the bedroom. But the girl knew Spoddy's common past and treated the letdown as a by-product of militarism.

"Honey," said she, in her paper-covers-rock voice, "if you'd only mush a bit. Unbend. Just don't haywire, like fucking is a pre-induction something." Pecking me.

"It's hard," I said, propped on right elbow. "For my fang is symbolized by this yard-long mackerel wrapped in brown rubber. When I salivate, the beasty slithers. Evil Companion, the Sorry Kid, and sixty-four thousand geniis insist on my loyalty to the regime."

Mystifications were inconsistent to Barbie. Girls fresh to default find the embankment slanted lightly. It is. However, in the negative universe there must be allowance made for sun, rain, clouds, crabweed, and flaws incarnate. Barbie wanted to seed my clouds and have electric storms. But a humble prong doesn't dress in karate pajamas, gothic sign (VISITORS 15 MINUTES A DAY), cut-of-line nostrils, the stagnation of Little Newark. My limitations and aspirations are hourly decimating.

I said: "If we rest awhile Barbie, and you comfort me . . . ?"

"The sick are a terrible burden," quoth she, stepping into those doeskin booties.

Anxious to keep THE SHOEDOG at bay, I shined my self with mustard. The spicy smell disorients the hound. "There's no need for you to split. And punishment's a stone drag. Meteors are God's punishment to man. Come here. I offer you as substitute an upside-down tongue."

She sat on the edge of the bed and guffawed, lush with condescension. "You're right, how can I say anything? You're the boy with the words. Use them, twist them, pervert them, mother them. Hurry and hustle words. Win an argument, win the lie. I can't take it no more. The patience factor climbs the wall."

Evil Companion — A NEIGHBOR BOY FOUND THE GAMMON LUSHY IN A SHED NEAR HIS HOME. WAKE UP TO FUR

Sun-down Magic Alice highstepped gold-white under Barbie's knees. I ruffled the cat against my forehead, had her tuft my eyebrows.

"Barbie, pick up on this. Plant me for a few days and we'll see what happens. I'll go macrobiotic and get healthy."

Our archetype remained at an impasse for two minutes. But you can't salute a stained flag indefinitely. My reluctant body was diffusing a pink light. I suggested a suave rebuttal: she denied my incapacity. Only the carnal was acceptable.

"You're not going to get laid. Want to sleep over anyhow?"

"No. Please walk me home."

We were to the door when Ira appeared. "Guess what: There's a real-live psychedelic movie being shown in the park. Come hither to celluloid spirals. Where's Mr. Funny?"

The four of us maundered thru the shade trees.

*   *   *

Hidden in Barbie's ear, "The park is weird. Who understands the stranger-dangers?"

"That," says she, "is because you're a soft-hearted and credulous person who wastes his time weaving leather aprons with Evil Companion and that repulsive juvenile. Hold my hand. Be affectionate."

Black thoughts wash the stream of people.

Change is foreseen.

Despite the darkness, all went well until we hit Birdcage Walk, the very center of Tompkins Square. Up ahead was a concentric circle of lumpen: ancient Yids, young spic hustlers bored blue in Amur'ka, and a motley degenerate host. They growled at the dragon nucleus. Shuddering as we approached, within a dozen yards of the scene I collapsed on the concrete and began davaning, hands around knees. "You can't flush a fascist, you can't make me go further . . .

Evil Companion — UNLAUGHABLE UNLAUGHABLES ARE MENTIONABLE UNMENTIONABLES ARE TOUCHABLE UNTOUCHABLES ARE VIETCONG STREET GANGS: UNEMBRACED SAVE IN RED AND BLACK MAGICK

. . . I won't go further," and hugged those knees, like a gargoyle in meditation.

For Spoddy's rarely outdoors. At this moment, here, now, the only Poem is Revolution. Reborn on plateaus, jungles of caution. Come tomorrow I got the chills. Come tomorrow be reintroduced to a Little Newark character called Crazed-Mit-Fear Arnie, an ex-rabbinical student turned gambler in the seedier nigger districts. If he didn't get his daily intimidation, it was a catatonic night. Once he approached a floating hash huddle and coming up the stairs to a first-floor apartment he heard laughter from behind a sealed door and drawn blinds. Crazed-Mit-Fear Arnie spent the next eight hours marching outside in the snow. Another head found him and wondered. Arnie shrilled: "You were giggling at *me*, at *me*, at *me!*"

Spoddy took uninsulated chances only.

"You chickenshit, Spoddy?" snickered Mr. Funny. "Birdcage Walk positively rivals the Haymarket with adorable people and hippies galore. Why," tearing a rose petal in half, "I come here for affection." Aromatic he was that night. Lilting. Intangible. I trusted his wisdom.

But in Amur'ka there should be sources of wisdom more alluring than the handicrafts of the blighted. Where are they? With a wee bit of courage, and the illustrious ability to absorb rays of love from the Van Allen Belt — *ALL IS ONE*. Down the path marched the Breather.

"Studs — are there any cosmic messages for me?"

My cozy group clung together, frozen in the nimbus of his consciousness. "The elves, people, are prancing from the vibrations of good loving. A happy consciousness is a happy man. Howdy." Sensitive to propaganda, Mr. Funny shimmied it jazzy and sidled to the Breather's side. Did a sycophant's duty.

"Here is a *beautiful* cat."

Adjectives working for you and the War's over. Soldiers come stumbling back and sow their crops on corporation turf. The banker is ghastly friend. Sell your daughter on credit. Will bends and sinks. Who needs the bow-legged piglet when you're dieting on lima beans forever? Wince at the StateSide gimp of the Leary. Munch the carpet till you're bleary. The War's over! The War's over?

Knowing he'd never hear those honest words in his lifetime the Breather asked: "Why you sitting on the temporal cold ground in that awful one-dimensional position?" As I tightened the grip on my knees, "Remember, Spoddy, to be beautiful to the physical world and it will in turn rectify the transcendental for you." He grinned girlish and limp, specialty of the conman bullshit mystic. "Who could get behind some portable enlightenment?" That question evoked moans of ecstatic assent in Tompkins Square. Mr. Funny made a daring grab for his mescaline tablets, and Ira offered him a starring role in his forthcoming cinematic epic — *Group Mind* — and everything was everything. Twilight is the time for East Side enchantment.

"Where's the focking film?" I wondered aloud in my churlish, unloving way. When the cosmic kids come scuffling my direction, can't reinforce the murmuring curtains of their egos, as if after acid, I mutiny internally. "Breather, Breather is an out-of-sight personage," said Mr. Funny. "I mean, he ought to be canonized. Last week he set the Statue of Liberty afloat with a kilo of gold . . . the iron lady took to it. Two days before a starling landed on his head, the mothering oven. He let it stay. Is it loony that the bird should nap off its busted wing on his head? Is it? My L–rd . . . ," commencing

Evil Companion — READ MORE IDEOGRAMS INEXCUSABLE. THE EASY BOX CONDENSES. LIBERATE DREAMS NOW

found Spoddy asking

endless trivia: "Where — o harbingers of configuration — is the Iron Necessity of Infantile Disorder? Where's the movie already? Where's the movie?"

"Past the threshold of void," said the 25 year old Breather, lank blonde hair lifting on a depraved city breeze, adding: "beyond the fierce sacrilege ahead." I let Barbie help me to my feet and hesitantly walked. The Breather worried about me, tried stuffing pills in my fist. "Swallow these Spoddy and breathe deeply, deeply. Get the bumpy rush, then arch the back and take more deep deep breaths. You'll love the feeling." Cleverly, I jammed the pills up my snout and we continued along Birdcage Walk. Decided to reach a bad end on my own time.

Skirting the tawdry mob scene of Spanish and Jewish origin, I heard a feminine shout: "The Mafia killed my old man! Used grease-guns on him and his guts was splashing over the blanket. THE MAFIA KILLED MY OLD MAN . . . !" in a refrain of endless terror.

The voice was familiar. "I believe that's Julia," I said, "your sister of the park." Heads swiveled as Barbie listened to an agonized, blistered shout: "Big Tuna and his rats killed Daddy, those pasty-faced rascals . . . !!" And my partner said, "Shouldn't we do something about it?"

"No."

Trees in Tompkins Square resemble leaky saleswomen doing religion. Urban clouds of smog engross you. Concerned with implosion, I hooked my arm around Barbie's waist, said: "Us — Barbie and Spoddy — is going to find a way to the forgotten truths."

She puckered young lips. "What are you talking about?"

I said: "The border of mystery, baby."

It dawdled, fashionable and coy, until the five of us discovered a grove of trees splintering off one of the park's many by-paths. Reluctant to persevere, middle-class youth doubting tomorrow, I implored Ira: "You're my friend for Life. This phosphorescent War and the Easy Box have boiled my heart for the last semester, as it were, so to speak. Should I chance the woods? Is it reliable?"

In disgust, Ira tore a wet branch from an aspen tree and began flagellating himself. There is no beginning. Tompkins Square Park was an element behind him. How many lost their grip here? "Yeah, put yourself on a bum trip Spoddy." His horsey face looked severe and ideal-istic at night. "Your trouble is hair-pie. And stop seeing life in semester units. Imagine it! A twenty-year-old man who ain't in school, on the job, in the army, not in jail, and he thinks of life like some Professor Darksocks Dubowitz in the stacks diddling his wire under the table, wow . . . ." He spit white gook in my face.

Mr. Funny: "Chickenshit, my roommate is . . . ."

56

Two ripe fists containing pills to overflowing were pushed under my nose. The Breather barked thru his blonde beard: "Pills! Don't you want no pills? Take pills and go USA contemporary. Don't you want to be contemporary? And breathe deeply up your left leg and out the right . . . ," from this retail spirit-monger.

Panic-stricken, I sprinted thru the park. Outlining the Square, guarding it like flaky hags waiting for the mortician's final ball, were the tenements of my peers. The bright moon was littered with Great Power's masturbation moonshots. This bright moon revealed mental quicksilver

Evil Companion — SPODDY, SO-CALLED, DRIPPED CANDY SPOTS ON CITY STREETS. THIS IS DEBRIS. YES, WE MEAN THAT OUR SOULS WILL BE FOREVER NAKED TO ONE ENORMOUS EYE OF TRUTH AND JOY

and I dodged the trash baskets, running out to 10th Street, streaking off to Avenue Q, running left to Baltimore, howling off to Los Angeles and the Dopey Lovers, peetering a moment in Elkorn, Nevada's ice-tong doctor offices, economizing on the half-fare return flight to

Evil Companion — DESTROY THE MUSEUMS, LET THE STRUGGLE BEGIN

and the crunch of her angry crotch.

6 / A Stranger Duet

Back in the living room, weary from these common journeys, I sipped Leapfrog Milk. It puzzles Spoddy not at all how Amur'ka mass produces millions of fresh juiceheads per annum. Must be they're dying like flies in Asia.

I'm sipping this Leapfrog Milk and it makes olfactory delight. Cherries and tapioca and ginger-ale and coffee with a fizzle of whipped cream on top. It's his favorite drink and Spoddy looks yummy drinking this confection, in the burgundy poorboy sweater with the high collar, and the proud long hair a-linkin' in the breeze romantic, and his blubbery lips a-saggin' to his knees, and his ears agin' his head like they was crucified by the transistor kings. Beautiful and loved, as the old daddy put it.

"Laying in front the telly and reading them comic magazines again. Gimme!"

"I'll give you," — rolling his EYEBROW MEETS THE NO-NOSE FOURSOME booklet around a lead pipe cerebral excursion — ". . . so I'm a pop-off, huh? Time you got reasons for the petty bourgeois hangups. Take this . . . !" and the pipe splits his skull with a sound of how do you make an Italian? You take a ripe tomato and you find a wall and you toss this tomato and WOP!! you got yourself a crime cancer carrier, except for Mario, the guys at the candy-store, and the anonymous old Sicilian who fills the gumball machine.

"You got (grunt) money for drugs, huh? You got money (grunt-grunt) for those goofy bananas, right? You got coin for the (000-grunt) beguilement of baby-dress styling . . . in the — ahh — grown-up chic of ever-pleated polyester chiffon and (grunt) coin for tent-tempting velveteen blouses of which there are 200 in the closet and money for records money for pot-pot-pot, and lottsa (grunt) lottsa money, right . . . ?"

"Grind it harder Daddy hardddderrrrr . . . ."

So these mediocrities are emitting static for a glass Leapfrog Milk, drink necessitating Monastic Way. It reminded me of a group Little Newark exotics decided to get 'awayfromitALL' and they move to prairie and build huts, carve dipshit knick-knacks, write trash, and erect hungry antennae to watch television from all over the world. And soon boredom with HIGH sets in and they a 7th St. return desire but the brown-rice fans are testing testing and the television becomes forgotten mommy . . . they dry to zombies; doorbell — clue to fresh orgasm with the universe — rings in Spoddy's Fuse House.

Bihder brothers troop in, lounge on bench and hammock. Heads longer than wide, white fangs gleam, and inside wraparound shades they sting me like Owners With A Proposition.

"Hi, how are you? We like, like to bite. We're Bihders. Bite with us?"

Franz B. is scratching his glazed jaw, sunk tissue-paper shit in the hammock.

Spoddy walks to the window, digs the herky-jerky alley below. Spics stand a chance? I cried: "The lights enslave! We call the night! We the breathing strong citizens must control the power plants! The mind is ancient! An ocean! Wage slavery prisons, police, armies must return to the bestial swamp of their origin! The wheels turn! Soon the lights will dim again! Ready?"

Franz removes wraparound shades to reveal gluttonish greedeyes. Eliminates doubt: "We like to bite, only to bite. Landed our copters on the roof. Follow . . . ."

We three take the trap-door route to tenement 7th Street tar/roof. Above 14th Street is turmoil. Midget helicopters have fangs painted in luminous red upon them. Names — Jolly Gumbo and Jumbo Folly. Puzzle page in my newspaper. Said: "Mine is the anarchy of simple forces. Sex hunger thirst. Let's blast this festering system."

The Urge to be a pioneer.

The Urge to be a prophet.

The Urge to be a plant.

The Urge to be a planet.

Spoddy and the lean demons swept thru the clouds, dangling egos behind, shredded veins. Over Little Newark, over ruptured metropolis. Spoddy joyful in the airwaves: you shoulda seen us. Each time we have a quarrel, it breaks my heart. But I realized gendarme-style incidents are occurring when we disend into forest preserve called golf course. Woody rhymes. Hills. Sandpits. Fat men in go-carts. Eden in northern New Jersey.

Suspicious Spoddy: "We'll snatch pussy on a golf course?"

The choppers flurried a dirt storm landing. We coughed, we fled from Jolly Gumbo and Jumbo Folly, resting under an oak tree on the grass. Lay there wheezing, vomiting yellow jam. "What the fock is the meaning of this?" cried Spoddy, outraged.

To hell with imperialist war now.

To hell with peaceful coexistence.

Just then the underbrush surrounding us crackled with boots and flailed machete. Lieutenant Pocoloo stuck his pumpkin out from behind a mulberry bush. His head was bound in bloody rags like a Revolutionary War veteran. Bihder brothers chant: "Hi . . . . He's a hostage delivered. Bye now. We like —."

"Certainly, sirs. Here's your ransom."

He squatted over exhausted me, probed my corneas with opal flashlight. Blinded Spoddy a moment. Then he looked at the helicopters, sagging there, motors pulsing. They were side by side.

"Sorry Mam," says he, "you'll have to move your genitals off the road. I'm here to look for the SHOE-DOG."

The lieutenant took the bayonet off his carbine and stuck it thru my black orlon turtleneck, my burgundy poorboy sweater, my baby-blue jacket, and drew blood. The sharpy-sharp point punctured my clavicle. Dark red flowed down my chest.

But Spoddy fixed his lights on the soldier's nose.

"Stop staring!"

But Spoddy fixed his lights on the soldier's heart.

"Coward!"

He was furious and raised the bayonet for another rape. Yet Spoddy got his Evil Companion secrets and astral-projected his own self inside the militarist's body. That surprised him. O brothers and sisters of the sinister path, that laid the old man low. "Where'd the double-crossing hippy go?" Fit my self neatly within, snug from fingertips to kneecaps never kneeled. And, believe it or no, the gold course from behind his orbs was shaggier than from behind Spoddy's. Hyperbole hairless spiders were engines in his brain. I began to rock/roll around white corpuscles

62

Evil Companion — YOU'RE ALL RIFF.
KEEP WORKING, KEEP

            leading Lieutenant Pocoloo to his first hard-on in horizontal decade.

Puffed and perspired.

Made his lips say: "OoOoOoOoOoOO, meow." It was moist, pelican, chalk-white elephant inside Pocoloo. The sun was prickly, nagging on his bandages. I was bored shitless so cloistered. Then Spoddy jumped out of Lieutenant Pocoloo, appearing face-first before his face.

"What'd you think of that?" Wound began to trickle again, and The Pain was there.

His putty-colored flesh was inflamed. He watched the Bihder brothers soar into paper clouds, licked his lips, shouldered the rifle, said: "Something happened which I don't understand." Astounded, he hoisted his rifle, aimed it again at my clavicle ". . . won't shoot if you tell me how you did it."

Evil Companion the Magnificent!

Evil Companion the Lufi!

Evil Companion the Scorch!

7 / White Clavicle and Son

Monographs were written to elucidate the phenomena. Like: THE COLLEGE DROPOUT AND THE REGENERATION OF NEUROTIC WOE, by a council of Park Avenue elders. Spoddy was a half-ass drifter reading it in his dusty house.

"Yes . . . whip, coerce, and suspend your child's allowance to send 'it' back to the college of his choice — the *best* college of his choice, of course. And he better tell all his one-armed hip friends about it. Purely for more knowledge, naturally. Mention the Depression Years six times in fifteen minutes. Rebuke him for his doped-up fucked-up look. Rebuke him with an anecdote of the Blumenthal child currently coasting across Morocco atop his hyena, Calvin, wasted out of his box on belladonna and skag. Does your child have a future? Will the subway robots be calling him BOY till he drops? Is it good karma?"

Intrigued, Spoddy read on:

"When referring to your child's career, avoid the word 'job.' Numerous dropout males, devoid of technological ego capacities, are subject to hysterical fits upon hearing this harmless vowel-consonant combination. The Blumenthal freak, for instance, after his father said — 'It's the *job* of any government that respects its werewolf junky priests to sterilize your baby sister' — held his breath until he turned blue, ingested 500 micrograms of psilocybin, mounted Calvin, and was taken into custody three days later praying to a radiator which he said emitted 'a fiery white light which indicates your assorted ground actions suck raisin extract and I'll never go back to Yale!' The worried parents phoned me and . . . ."

I digested the tract in a matter of mini-seconds compared to the life of a star (which is all you is) and accompanied Liz the localized troll to the Saint Boz Orphanage in search of solace. We walked a yellow lawn flanked by pastel-blue trees. Sunday afternoon upset Liz: "Treat your boy Jason like a precious package." This witch, this member of the cozy body of Christ, was riffing to me of okies in the Ford plant

Evil Companion — THOSE SIDEWALK CANDY SPOTS ARE AN UGLY BLOTCH. A CLEANER VOID IS UP TO

her ominous, pinched brow, "You brought flesh and blood into this nasty world Spoddy. Stick by that sperm!" I didn't anticipate concern in a girl so dipsy. Her story: "Like my application in the Ford plant read 'And how many hours do you plan to *devote* to the Ford plant?' causing me to split. My life's been a series of startled floor-walkers."

"And what could *you* do in a Ford plant?" We were nearing the orphanage, a brick building with turrets. The sun razed the silhouettes of the nuns manning the guardwalks. Swaths of black cloth dragged the brick edges.

"No chicken-hearted jurors these," I said.

Liz the localized troll was bitter. "19 years old and my face is wrinkled sad. I'm a permanent enemy of those mutilating motherless youth."

On the orphanage grounds, ambling over the yellow lawn. Knots of orphans AC-DC ran towards us, shouting invective in the granulated accents of the poor. I took a handful of dimes from Spoddy's pocket and scattered them around me, like a Rockefeller monster deceased, asking a freckled/redheaded tot: "Say, where's my kid — Jason?"

The boy glared. "Who's your kid, mister? We're orphans. What's this crap with 'my kid?' We're forked worm orphans our life away." He signaled a hefty tyke in short pants and muscle t-shirt. "Hey Pocket Veto! C'mere." An orphanage bullyboy approached, probably the illegitimate son of a Little Newark wop gambler. Havoc in the city, he'd infiltrated the sole Yiddish-speaking bookie and pasted his nose upside his head. "This longnosed bastard wants his kid, Pockets." A small mob of children was foaming around us. They had long arms and short pockets. They had short arms and long pockets. The redhead, high as my waist, pulled off his undershirt to probe his belly-button for lint. "Now," he whimpered slowly, "takin' all angles inna question, how could he find his boy considering we're orphans?" Enraged, he flung his undershirt to the ground and stomped on it, shouting: "I'll kick your ass! The fucking insult of it!!"

"Easy does it," said Liz the localized troll. "We're good people. Mr. Spoddy meant not his son but his nephew, Jason." Grateful, I decided to no longer dilute her acid with meth. This was a bad habit.

"Witch! Stone the witch!" The waif called Pocket Veto grabbed Liz around the boobs and wrestled her to the ground. She screamed dirty lightning. Grunting like a Serbian Alderman, he attempted impregnation. U.S. troops reported killing 32 Viet Cong just south of the demilitarized zone, namely your genitalia and amigos. Kids lobbed rocks. A brick chunk hit my chin and I wasn't even

Evil Companion — WHO INVENTED BAILIFFS? WHO INVENTED NATIONAL BOUNDARIES? WHO CRAVES COMFORT ABOVE LOVE? LURE ONE INTO THE CLOAKROOM. OFFER FEET. OFFER FINGERS. OFFER $ TO SUBVERT GREEDS TO NEEDS. BURN BUSES BEHIND STP. GET

incite the playground. Is her body a
threat? Still impotent after your 30th acid trip? Reading more? Digging dope less? Big shit that Dong Lee a
five year old South Vietnamese girl learned to smile
again with no nose? With no nose? With no nose? Robert Louis Stevenson loathed human snouts. He'd pick
up on a black great-coated burghermeister, say: "How
did that most sordid piece of human nature, that jiveass
motherfucker, get such whangdang in the vortex of did
you tabulate it a FACE!?" So I kicked Pocket Veto soggy
pink bullshit (who by this time repeated boyishly —
"Witch smell like dada sandalwood . . . Witch smell like
dada sandalwood") and — pulling Liz behind — raced
toward the main building, the guard towers. Hilarious
crowd of orphans and scholars chased us, flinging EN-
CYCLICAL O and other misinterpreted bestsellers.

Refuge was a distance off. I dodged among see-saws
and sandboxes, cracking Liz ahead of me like in Vir-
ginia Reel. The orphan vigilantes traveled buckshot
fashion, tried to surround us. Glib paranoia. Chased by
children. Chased by

TIME TIME TIME TIME IS A CLOT IN
THE THROAT OF ETERNITY

and Pocket Veto shortcutted,
wheel of destruction and creation before us, holding a

68

baseball bat, luminous with hate. Crisis dynamite wrapped in plastic bags. Suddenly a shot rang out and Pocket Veto screamed: ". . . de Choich shot me, OOO! I'm hit, OOOOOOOO!" whirling pogo-sticky to the grass as in the game who-falls-the-best played in vacant lots the world over. His wee body lay spread-eagled still. The other waifs vanished.

Squatting to administer, Spoddy was surprised to hear this severe woman's grunt: "Get your hands away sir, if you will." It was a nun carrying a chocolate submachine-gun at my rent in arrears. She was in the middle of her life. She had the coiled rubbery face of a Little Newark waitress denying ricepudding to the after-midnight winos . . . "I'm a hobo, sir. I've been a hobo since '61. My wife was a nurse at Grand Central Station. Since she died, sir, I've been bo-ing in this most psychotic of all cultures since B.C. begun. Spare a cigarette sir? Spare three cigarettes, sir? I'm fifty-six years old and I've done it everywhere. I'm a nigger. I boxed with Joe Louis and Sugar Ray in the army. Look in my eyes. They go TWINKLE!! even now. Who's keeping score? Who's keeping score of my misery? Who's scoring twenty million crushed nigger souls while you eat overpriced macrobiotic dinners in the restaurant with the good vibrations? Still eating? Still eating?" . . . and baby I jest of pushups in the cucumber patch, but Firbank ain't shit. Never met a fag ain't out for the dollar.

"You plugged that lithe youngster!" cried Liz the localized troll. This weren't a low-level hippie chick shrieking O WOW & GROOVY till you vomit, but the granddaughter in spirit and flesh of a leatherworker sweeping Cossacks off holy ponies in 1905 revolution. A family saga behind her eastside/tired/gaunt/pale/Central European face smeared dirty, no earrings. Three brothers flee Tsarist police, hitch-hike by Alaskan raspberries, settle in Brownsville. Uncle Meyer is 81 and still a Party pimp . . . "He woiks for de Staid Deportmunt. Don' believe a woid. Abram Tertz was a social fascist. Gimme anudder pickle." . . . Uncle Saul is 73, organized the Fur Workers, social democrat . . . "State capitalism is hypnosis. Gimme anudder pickle." . . . Uncle Monk is 70, hung tight with Lepke dead — alas! — these twenty years . . . "Snatch another pickle and you'll wind up fertilizer on my Lakewood, New Jersey chicken farm of nigh onto 20,000 acres." Clichés, more clichés, all I hear is etc.

"Mr. Funny, with those posies behind your ear you look like a goddess. I love you!"

"Demi, my dear, only demi."

"Mr. Funny, how come a cat like you hangs with such a lame clique of ultra-sophisticated New York City coterie fag poets what haven't raved one ego-perverseless inch?"

"Since you've swallowed all that acid, you've become even more adjectivized. Unbutton your bellbutton-bottoms. I'm out for bland dinner."

"My cock tastes bland?"

"All cock tastes bland."

Liz the localized troll is a tough chick. She looked, now, haggard and bemused. She had some mescaline in her and smiled the guardhouse nun ashes. "Why'd you shoot that lithe orphan youngster?"

The nun fingered her rosary before answering. "This m'lad," said she to me, "is a CO2 pellet gun. New type of disciplinary weapon. From that Haight," gesturing with chocolate barrel at a guard-turret, "it merely stuns. He's feigning death as Marxist kids often do." Prodding the boy by means of edible weapon, all weapons edible: "Rise and ritualize you bastard before I . . . !"

Jack-in-the-box to his feet. "Excuse me, Sister Marie. I'm going to trundle . . . ," and tried to dash. But she quickly pliered an earlobe.

"Listen, you heretical twerp . . . where's the DMT you and that lugubrious pal of yours got hid? In the name of a thousand and one dimensions, where is it?" She twisted his hot wax ear into an S-shape.

Point of ravaged order. "O!"

*   *   *

I'll tell you why I'm down on queers. It's because

71

when I was in highschool I mess around alot and this homeroom teacher named Mrs. Deutch got uptight because I wouldn't salute the flag and I got sent down took a fall suspended and sent to this wacked out guidance center for kids downtown where I met again all these groovy racist Italian and Irish kids I grew up in that neighborhood Vailsburg in west Little Newark and those fuckers were mean — Wow! — those were mean guys like Jimmy Lavitola I had a crush on him in sixth grade his father watered the elephants for Ringling Brothers he's in Bordentown for felonious assault you people get high alot and think you know where it's at but that's bullshit because I was getting high at twelve years old they called me The Baby Viper me and this cat Jacky Jones bet you didn't know a spade won't sell dooshy to a cat named Jack Jones its tied up with mojo roots . . . . Well I hung in this candystore named Stein's and at ten-thirty me and Jacky and Richy Shwartz walked around the block sipping wine and puffing joints then down to the movies to pick up on the chicks this guidance counselor really fucked me up because when I went to see him I'd rather look like a hood then a hippy-dippy street person anyday the fucking faggots. This guidance counselor seduced me no shit invites me eat dinner yeah eat dinner I know I know *eat* and *dinner* but he made me come back to his office where the couch unfolded to a bed and he d—, he . . . .

I'll tell you why I'm down on queers. They're trying to get off easy I mean chicks don't have to do shit but lie there white wide and moaning on summertime butts and these faggots got hip to the difficulty of hardons so they lay there and some wear dresses while a stud like me balls 'em the fucking faggots you can't walk thru a park without some sweet stuff trying to seduce you. Is it clear? Am I making sense? Maybe I'm wrong I admit I could be wrong but these faggots are unnerving it's all right if they were quiet about it but take a fag like Capoot he's like a eunuch Jacky Onanass walks around and Warhog so mercenary makes a thousand a week from movies it's a new race of castrati it's the civilization what does it turns men against women black against white young against old and he made me come back to his office where the couch unfolded to a bed and he d—, she . . . .

*   *   *

I'll tell you why I'm down on queers. He said, "I'm a *mocker*. You and your candy bars leave me house." Is that weakness? I mean it's a drag his uncle fucked Gide but do you think it's weak? I do. I think it's sick no matter what.

*   *   *

73

Satiated, Sister Marie released the boy — eyed Liz contemptuously — and intimated that we should follow her to the central compound.

This main orphanage construction was Victorian tiled. Global the sandy stink of naptime, holy water, and russet graham crackers. Pint milk cartons and catechism booklets littered my eyeballs, the halls. We were led by Sister Marie

NO TOTALITY IMPRESSING THE GREAT SHOEDOG. RADIO PHOTO OF YOUR KNOWLEDGE SURMISE

to an austere office.

"Be seated," said she. 'I'll get the Mother Superior." She left thru a limp bead curtain, trailing a tunafish gas.

"This is stupid," I said to Liz. "Nuns used to pinch me on Little Newark's Sanford Avenue. And there's a paucity of that vital Boystown elan here. My son, Jason, will come and despise me in the traditional father/son U.S.A. relationship. Maladjusted, you'll see . . . ."

She smiled her horsefeather smile. "Responsibility's the word Spoddy. Lemme tell you how the goyim ball chickens in the Ford plant. These hillbillys rut the bird and just about to orgasm they choke it to death. They call it in the Ford plant the 'dying ass quiver' . . . ."

The bead curtains parted.

"I heard that," cried Lieutenant Pocoloo, striding thru,

rapping a swagger stick against his pants leg. I vaulted to the door: barred by the bulk of Sister Marie, chocolate gat poised.

So I slumped back in the orange sling chair, novelty in the Mother Superior's office. The walls were pimpled with Jesuses in G-strings. Spoddy was resigned. "You're probably fed up with me," said the lieutenant. "But I've called you here on a matter of celestial importance. It's important why I called you . . . ," the bandages still looped his forehead, still wearing combat fatigues in the Saint Boz Orphanage. Frankly, I couldn't make head or tails of it. "Your picture, Mr. Spoddy, has been on television. The Texan seen it. Know what sin that means? The big bombers of Guam are underway — underway — and the sin of the plaster elf is buried in your granddaughter's dolly internals . . . ," he picked his nose, did the bubble inflation, puzzled. "Since you pushed me I've been defensive and paranoid and fumigated and hostile." To my contrary sight, he seemed deep-mellow yellow. High. "How's that, Spoddy? How's that?"

Sister Marie erect between us like stern dung, scowling. "Lieutenant, handle this hooligan properly. The Marxist kids are always there, skulking behind the window shades of your jawbone." Hers were lumpy/striped teeth and the curse of chewing out the confessional for hours. "Damn it!" She slammed the rifle butt into his chest like the La Guardia Civil puts down a clerical talkout. "In the name of the external Godhead, straighten out!" Was Liz the localized troll's turn to whisper urgently: "This nun atrocity's got four ankles."

"Christ, everything is a fog of words," the lieutenant was insisting/imploring as Sister Marie, weighing 180 pounds, drove him into a poontang corner. "I knife Spoddy in the clavicle — this dyke sticks me. Cut it," trying to shield himself from her relentless fury with the swagger stick, as in Chinee Short-Pole Fighting. I saw a pair of sneaker toes rent the Sister's blackhabit as she stalked.

"Gracias," to Liz for the tip.

"It's cool," said she. Seizing a bronze Mary-Our-Blessed-Mother-of-God paperweight, I busted Lieutenant Pocoloo's head.

(a mouldy pink canteloupe — tifftattoo — rushing brain seeds, flushy, across the floor in red/white carrots)

Then, that paperweight lovely, I busted Sister Marie's head — as in lethal Baltimore Boy Bolo Punch.

(A bloody red habit — tumtittaw — "the Pope's an elderly man running a large business organization" — spitting sausage sizzle, aglide the food in blue rivulets)

Evil Companion —

???   ???   ???

WALLPAPER ILLUSION OF GREEN EYES. BODY ILLUSION OF
URINE SPONGE ???

       I toppled, zonked, to the sling chair.

     *   *   *

 We trio sat tangled on the lawn of the St. Boz Orphanage, catching the rays of a corn-stalk sun. The
sound of orphans playing tag barely reached us. It was
a dry autumn. Indian Summer weather. My prodigal
sun, Jason was studying a sleeping Liz, twisting his
red cowlick, ignoring me. I plucked up, asked: "You
burned me for a dime of speed. Now you don't seem so
very glad to see me — my, my boy." I was reluctant to
acknowledge paternity. "You dig, we didn't recognize
you coming in a while ago. Your hair," stomach heaved
gently velvet glove, "it wasn't always red, was it?"

 He didn't reply, sullenly curled the cowlick.

 "What I meant was . . . ," and stopped. Seemed hope-
less to attempt rapport with this child I'd abandoned at
— was it seventeen? — just three years ago? Startled,
my jaw tumbled down and I drooled like a papier-maché
lover — this wasn't my four year old son.

 He clawed eyebrows.

 "You're a neurotic double motherfucker," he declared
so abruptly my jaw clanged metallic. "For the three
years I've been here I saw you come looking for your
son. What son? Where's your son? Two months ago

you came by with another girl, not this witch" — pointing to bedraggled Liz on the grass, her pocked legs gone fetal in sleep. "It was a pretty girl. Who was that girl? She had the sly body." Freckleface grinned, pre-puberty insinuation.

"Her name is Barbie."

He stared at the ground a moment, drew a slit trench with his toe. "My last name is Eppus. Joe Eppus." He passed me a groundglass mean look. "I got the last name, you dig? Not this Jasonshit." He rose and flung his arms apart, stretching an unripened chest. "Like I said when the sea casts up its nameless dead, you're a sick double motherfucker for real."

Why challenge this insipid someday acid freak? But did. "What jobs am I qualified for? You're — what is it today? Wednesday? — eleven?" Yet I was worried about his keyhole to my obsession. Some kids get vicious next to my closet stagnancy. If you're still out for revenge, join the Party. My lips only are chapped.

"Forget my age," he said. "I want to find stuff out. You interest me. I like to read on my hip. By oceans. By streams. Dig: if you look at Diamond Crystal Salt under a microscope, you will see that every grain has facets like a tiny diamond pecker. Unlike that old salt which looks like plain cubes and bounces off your snatch — still eating? — Diamond Crystal, the uncommon salt, has facets to cling. Stays when you shake it.

Salts evenly to bring out ALL the flavor. Makes food taste uncommonly wet. Try to pinch and feel. How come you come here to look for your son? You don't have a son." He hurled a brick 30 yards into a dance of girls doing hopscotch riddles, then sat anonymous during the painful shouts. "How come?"

The Saint Boz Orphanage had acres of fenced-in lawn for the detention of Eppus' comrades. I scanned the horizon of swirling children. Lost-face teardrops made me ashamed. "It does my libido a fictional warmness coming here, Joe. It drives Evil Companion to halls of justice." Plucking my adam's apple nervously: "You see, I'm a bum. I'm waiting for the concentration camps got a paint job in Arizona last spring. Is Europe a grave-yard? Why do the shaggy sadhus in amber robes and beads think they're stronger than Watts? Ever watch the merchants munch potato chips? You see, I'm a proud bum. Wasted in the evenings, dozing to late afternoon. Home is chemicals, War news, kicking the kitty. So the orphanage pleases me, as it were, so to speak." Realizing the head changes that signified: "I'm sorry, Joe."

He moved closer and draped a hand over suede shoulder.

"Your generation interests me," he declared softly. "Who is the 'evil companion' you mentioned? The devil? Your prick? A crooked cop? A black satanist?" Funny, his boy hand on the suede collar of Spoddy coat traded for a spoon of meth it gives you pimples, those tiny dungarees, those black/white sneakers I wear no more. "You seem messed up for a big guy. How come you fell in love with the completely subjective reality, the steel penis? How come you knock out the soldier and Sister Marie?"

Regained my guts. Kill a fly under LSD. Matter whether you do or don't? Is it all maya? Illusion? Five years in the joint for possession will teach truth. "I'll answer after you tell me why you were moonlighting under her cunt."

That kiddy rolled, laughing. "I was eating her out, you bucket-eyed lame."

We roared and thumped the ground. I affirmed, between guffaws, our oral proclivities. However, Liz the localized troll awoke and shook crumbled leaves from the valley of her skirt. She said: "It's 4:30 Spoddy. We shouldn't still be here. They going to find those two corpses and — BOOM! — we're busted."

"Shuddupandrowse."

Until she slept, Joe Eppus and I watched the evening wind tear among the branches. Piles of orange leaves, raked by waifs, dotted the peripheral visionary. Because we were nestled in a remote wooded area beyond the playing fields, among Indiana Mauve bushes, we weren't noticed by the nuns shepherding children back inside the dormitories. Spoddy washed his Great Face:

"I *like* you, man."

"It's mutual. You got the potential."

"Potential?"

He waved his fingers. "Yeah, you're so far out you couldn't rerun if you tried. All doors are closed. Yeah, you got the nice potential. Four, maybe five years you'll be delectable. But you've got to learn not to trust nobody. Not to trust COCK OF FAMOUS POET heading for India when his wife has a kid and the lovehippie myth. Nobody . . . ."

"I know where they're at."

Joe Eppus yawned, scratched his young nuts, and took some sticks of gum from windbreaker pocket. The kid was quip.

"Here. I like you. Lemme ask this. When you was my age, did you hide food around the plate? If you weren't hungry?"

Evil Companion — HERE I AM AND I'M BACK AGAIN

next thing Spoddy knew the boy was thrusting a Bible at me. "Ever read St. Peter? About how he too betrayed the Christ and then the tree, I think it was — NO! it was a cock — the cock crowed and Peter started crying. You ever read that?"

'Every question contains the answer.'

This third generation child wasn't five feet tall. He had red hair, freckles, face like a friendly SHOEDOG.

Why should I be reminded of the Wobblies? Was it because of the arms convention in the Chicago coachhouse with the warlord of the Stone Black Rangers, the chief thug of the Two-Penny Outlaws, the gunseller's son?

"I'm a functional illiterate."

Downed, he shook Liz conscious and prepared to leave. I wanted this thing to end casual. I got really predictable and offered him three sticks of tea.

"What's that? Red?"

"Homegrown. Try one. But don't oversquat: you'll fall in."

He backed off, cautious.

"Ney, ney. Like a horsey I say ney, ney."

Spoddy didn't expect from one so fresh and lively a come-to-Jesus torture. Christ did it one way, but too bloody. It's like the Aztec human sacrifice. If ten thousand people believe a stone axe in the heart will Enlighten, it'll Enlighten. "Listen Joey," and I sung:

"Long-haired preachers come out ev'ry night,
Try to tell you what's wrong and what's right,
But when asked about something to eat,
They will answer with voices so sweet:
'You will eat (you will eat),
Bye and bye (bye and bye),
In that glorious land in the sky (way up high).

Work and pray (work and pray),
Live on hay (live on hay),
You'll get pie in the sky
When you die (that's a lie!)'

but that's called levitation-of-a-minor, a felony in nine states.

"We're leaving. We're never coming back."

He complied: "Too bad." Laughing wildly little boy, he said: "Come and see me again. I'll take you to a hideout upstate, an anarchist rest home."

"Sure."

       Evil Companion — HERE I AM AND I'M BACK AGAIN

     walking Liz into the twilight, I snipped a wire-fence corner and invoked Little Newark

                      N O B O D Y
WANTS TO HEAR YOUR HEADY LINKAGES — Evil Companion

     and that made my right fist paralyzed for six weeks. Soaking the hand in New Left hell-broth didn't help.

DMT smoking caused it.

        *   *   *

A professor of rightwing socialist tendencies and his boy prodigy are playing chess:

"Young man, you've got to plug them in before you get a reaction. Our magazine functions as a mirror for their misunderstandings."

But the boy prodigy has met THE SHOEDOG.

"I dunno. Can't I withdraw before I'm mated? Can't I do that? Withdrawal before I'm mated, that's all . . . ."

"No!! You've got to play to the end!!"

"I dunno. This face I met name of THE GREAT SHOEDOG OF THE NORTHERN SKY gimme a cap pistol . . . ."

They both went away for a while.

8 / Elemental Possessions of Breather

We dined in the KOLOSSAL HEROES restaurant.

"Gassed to know you in this capacity," smiled the Breather, mitting me across salami crusts, the coffee cup debris. "I'm already on my third passport. When I was in Paris some scum A-rabs bought the other two. In the Algerian quarter."

An Italian waitress, pointy chin, beak nose, came to our table: "We don't have no brown rice. Who's got brown rice where there's heroes? You come here every day and ask for brown rice and then do the cheese 'n sausage. What is this shit?" She queried me, beehive hairdo like archaic plasterbomb, "There are meatballs in this neighborhood who ask for brown rice and won't settle for noodles. What causes it?"

Spoddy shrugged: the Breather said, "Leave us at once. I'm getting the hostile wop aura. I'll chant re-entry sutras." As her black uniformed bottom flounced thru the tables angrily, I underlined our deal redundant. "So it's settled. For each passport you get me I fork up $100, OK?"

"Right, right," said he, wiggling his hand as if to dismiss the grossness of the whole affair. "What interests me more Spoddy, is your newfound desire to get documents. You're going to sell them for enormous profits in Africa and who knew you're going . . . ?"

Ira came thru the door, redundant in floral vest and combat boots, carrying a cannister of film. He announced: "What a parody I completed! It shows the Secretary of State blowing an elk and a sign saying SO GLAD WE MADE IT pops out the elk's dick." He screamed to the waitress lounging at the counter over coke and The National Enquirer: "No more War for Profits! No more Peace for Tyrants!" To us: "I'm going too. The mind states stateside are too much for my waxy mind. The War, the stop 'n search thing. Always anxious, wrecked highs." Plopped beside me in the booth.

"Yeah," said the Breather, "it's getting more uptight these days of napalm woe." Looking mournfully out the window — cops, dopers, the usual grim array so lovely to describe — he flicked the contents of his right nostril to the doorway. Niggling farfetcher I'd label the Breather. Blonde beard, cookie-duster blonde mustachio, layover blonde/red hair, warmed by his burnoose in summer. "Spoddy, Morocco's the place. Just lay on your ass and smoke. I'm gonna distribute acid to the Berbers in return for art. Is your life ruined?"

Dunking a crust in my coffee, said: "Seen these sandwiches called submarines, torpedoes, garibaldis, hoagies, but only in NYC they're called KOLOSSAL HE-

ROES. Are we heroes? Do nothing but heroes live here?"

The Breather filled his char-lungs and gave me a fact-finding look. So dirty I blanched. "Spoddy, Spoddy, you're a typical unfree political dude. Shame. Here I'm scoring passports for you to sell at $1500 apiece, something I'm doing thru love for you, and you come on so strong I could plotz. Man!! what binds us youth today is love, you dig, L-O-V-E." Exasperated, he whipped one knee over the other triple times. "I figure jive from the DC savages, Spoddy. From you, never."

Evil Companion napped: Spoddy decided to argue.

"You suck. What binds us is hatred — intense, rosy hatred for our lot. H-A-T-R-E-D. Do I make myself ugly?"

The Breather moved his 225 lb. ex-football player from the University of Pennsylvania frame over the table and whispered: "Your 'self,' Spoddy? No, your 'self' ain't ugly. What's ugly," pausing to rap out a cigarette, "is your motherloving fear of cunt and the grave. Watch this proof."

Took from a stitched-in pocket of his burnoose a pink tissue and a safety-pin. He affixed the tissue to the pin-point, fluttering it gently.

"Look at this. I can turn it clockwise or counterclockwise with just my mind."

Stared at the paper flag. Nothing nothing nothing.

"I can turn it six ways with my eyes. You can too.

87

It's the power of L-O-V-E."

Ira was enthusiastic: "I can see it! I can make the tissue move!" Evil Companion —

HIPPIE POWER IS THE SUNSET STRIP TRIPPERS DETONATING ATOMIC DEVICES ON ACCOUNT THEY GOOF THE PRETTY PINK SUNSETS

which is chockful of psychedelic lore. And who is Spoddy to piss on kaleidoscopes? When is thought? And is that a black velvet dill-doll you got strapped on? And if your kidneys take ten tokes ten times one night, you'll be set straight? And does Vitamin B in the vein give you a 'nice, warm glow'?

These were some of the land turtles stampeding across my brain that hot afternoon. I decided, unadulterated by an articulate EC, to test his ingenuity.

"Prove it more. Prove it's love."

Breather hugged his burnoose tighter around him, clouding his face. Tuft of blonde mustachio peeked out.

"Ever shot any DMT?"

*   *   *

Twining among frog ponds, the Breather led the way. His blonde hair ebbed to streaky orange filaments. We walked the woods of Red Mountain. It was nighttime and I dug the scenery, the hundred hidden toad-croaks. Last in line, Ira ahead, Spoddy said irrelevancies to lance the amplified throats of beasties: "Sounds like the new jazz. Is that philistine or ain't it? Breather, with that lantern casting its yellow light you look like Arno the Boy Pirate. Know what I mean?" He turned and held the lantern above our heads, the flickering yellow draping us like a luminous cloak Barbie often wore. Was another permeation stare he gave me.

"Be quieter." Pointing to a screened-in cottage off to our left, he said: "The people who're letting me stay here are beautiful people, authenticated pious souls. But they don't know nothing about my — erh — artifacts in the woodshed. If you trouble, breathe up your left leg and out the right."

He moved forward again, leading us by lantern-light further into the woods. Entering a realm of primarily pine, he abruptly stopped and Ira bumped him.

"O excuse excuse."

"Forget it."

The Breather crouched before a maimed tree. Pried apart a cache of rocks, shone the lantern on a treasure-chest of my fears since nine years old.

Boast: "The stash inside, my friends, is worth a fortune on the teeny-tit market."

Finally intruded a cathedral of pine trees. These trees enclosed a bed of silky pine needles half a foot thick. I flung a tortured body down. Pine trees sprout fences on teenage vocabulary. It leaned lovely, the Red Mountain upstate forest. Understood now why the Breather kept an answering service to coordinate his cortical activities on weekdays. Cleanest psychedelic dealer in the business, unlike Spoddy rushing to and fro in a frenzy of imprecision . . .

The Scene — A bare empty room which constantly sort of hovers over any area that the occupants simultaneously wish. In walk Marcel Proust and Ernest Hemingway. It doesn't matter what periods of their lives either of them are from. They are damned in hell together.

Hemingway: You ever go swan hunting?

Proust: I beg your pardon?

Hemingway: Swan hunting?

Proust (paranoid)*:* Are you mocking me?

Hemingway: No, no, the bird. (pause) Look, don't get like that already. (pause) You know, the bird . . . swan . . . . (pause) They're wonderful to hunt, in Spain. Have you ever been in Spain? Their wine is very good. You drink it out of leather bags. The wine is excellent. You pour it —

Proust: Do you know where we might obtain some cork?

Hemingway: Cork?

Proust: Yes, cork; it would be of good use in sound-proofing the room to which we seem to be consigned, like a rat to its hole. (NB: Proust is the only man ever to speak in semi-colons)

Hemingway: You know, some day we have to go hunting in Spain. Or Africa. Or Big Two-Hearted River. I can teach you to tie flies. They struggle and try to get off the hooks, but they never can and the big fish get them. You get the big fish. (Long pause. Proust sneaks up from underneath Ernest and fondles his balls. Ernest visualizes a whole atrocious future of living with this queer, and goes mad. He displaces his personality as follows) I write columns for the Voice I'm Mailer I'm Hemingway for president fuck off you goddamn queen or I'll get you sent up like my 6 ex-wives and besides I can criticize destructively *any* work of literature ever written for Esquire watch out or I'll expose you, I'm the King of the Jews and you're only half Jewish, let me tell you about a wild party I was where we all went out to a Wisconsin dairy farm and gang-banged a cow . . . . I'm a failure. But I can always begin again.

. . . dragged a wake of offended customers behind me. Dealing dope has incipient glamor, but it quickly dissipates. Another common experience.

The bell of pine trees jabbed white clouds on blue sky. For each star raw, thousands cook. I said: "This where you make it when it rains?" Adding, "Your sex life — reprehensibly — is none of my business."

He pissed into the stream, not hearing, not caring.

To Ira: "You're being awful still. Ever been here before?"

He sat toasty beside me, dived eagle-on-rat into my eyes.

"Never made it. And you should consider how some eastern folks wipe their holes with left hands. ACHHANU HOLLAGADOO, he's got equipment and studio connections . . . ." Glancing over his shoulder, back to me. "Now Spoddy, I haven't seen you lift your veil lightly, those actor quirks come thickening, like if evil companion was thrilling you. You've got the mysterious mind. Don't," smoke curled shoulder, "don't go offending Him. The cat's a guru. He can teach you mucho. I mean," taking a figure 8 shaped breath, "I've gotten *high* mothajumpa *hiiighh* . . . ." Evil Companion —

SHE IS IMPATIENT TO GO TO HER HUSBAND, FOR THIS IS THE NIGHT OF

Spoddy was piqued at this trumpet: "How you expect me uncynical? Axe to the root, you lame, it takes an axe to the Pentagon's root."

Breather unfolded a sleeping bag, shielded the lantern with his burnoose.

"Rest, m'boy, dwell with the moon and stars."

And as the lantern's rays penetrated the bookbinder-blue sky, asked: "Arno — Arno the Boy Pirate. Don'chya recall? Gypsies caught him and he ate cheese fried on a sword in daguerreotypes, wore a St. Boz medallion. About ten years old and running away . . . . Fourth grade," I mused. "Does he ring, tear loose the knot of this world?"

Busy with syringe, he replied: "No. Listen, you've smoked this chemical, right?"

Got Spoddy irked, snubbing a press for camaraderie. All my friends got the mysterious mind: Man-against-Machinegun illiteracy is the 11th Street mystic's ailment. I sensed, too, the PONY UP ASS PONY UNDER DOG populations of GREAT SHOEDOG. Sniffed the GREAT SHOEDOG'S spoor. It smelled like blood/water/sodium pentothal — first baby baptism.

"Yeah, I've smoked. Sex goes swimming. Marveled at the lost opportunities for job and family."

"You're confused," he said. "This is bigger than acid. It irrevocably will alter your life. From the cowardly naive cynicism you beef about — from this tenth-rate involvement in Amur'kn horseshit," and here his arms spread wide enough to embrace the I Won't Work, "to an immensity of spiritual wholeness. Your politics will be God's politics."

Ira used his raspberry tie to belt me. But as the Breather tapped the spike into left elbow pit, the torn-

dollar collar slipped. Liquid splashed my wrist. "Damn,
he cried, "a good $^1/_2$ c.c. of God's sweat wasted." Not
quite: he'd squeezed the dropper. I implored the woods.
Pine trees shuddered: mutty faces. Lightly I insisted
". . . no big t'ing."

"It *is!* It *is* a big thing. Too much leaked out is all."
While he prepared the next injection, I wonder: "Can't
we do it by that gurgly stream?" He chuckled sagely:
"You dig, Spoddy, this ain't a mere sensory awakener
like LSD. It's astro-reality you're entering. Stars and
stripes. God as my everlasting witness, you'll adore it."

Jive Mind is ugly.

Jive Mind is feeble.

He stuck me, the night wind competing with corporation hootowls, bats swooping low over the lantern,
and the Red Mountain stream squizzled. Ira held the
lantern closely-close so Breather could see blood-
threads float in the dropper. Spoddy licked the red pearl
after . . . .

Five seconds silence. Then my lungs racked.

"Ah," chuckleheaded the Breather, satisfied, "the tell-
tale cough." He pushed my shoulders. "Lie back
Spoddy, stretch on the sleeping bag."

Ira was lucid. "Have a nice time out there."

*   *   *

Cultureless: concentric pink circles ejaculate thru

	a dome in mind. Electric devils ride global blue bicycles. Music of the Spheres. It hasn't been sculpted/ filmed/ written/ fucked/ digested/ made perfidious/ remembered.
Stateless:	concentric Pink Snakes undulate thru spent Flesh. Flying saucers are clinical and aloof. I can be cowed/ worshipped/ voted/ weather-proofed/ done in/ Decembered.
Fatherless:	Please me.
Fruitless:	Consolidate imaginary gains.

*   *   *

For forty clocked minutes

LOYALTY TO THIS GEN-
ERATION — Evil Companion

and then I sat.
"Wheeeeeew . . ." at seeing the top of Ira's head extended to a quivering/shimmering arrowpoint, and
— mother subtracts child — put Spoddy's moist face
next to Ira's knee.

"Does it end?"

He hugged me pretentious. "Courage!"

"Does it end? Does it end? Does it end? Does it end?
Does it ever end?" The forty scorched minutes but an
instant and he said the wrong thing:

"It'll always be a little with you. Go to it."

Gripping his knee, to acknowledge the dead-fact mind-fucking corduroy. "But will it end *now?*"

The Breather chimed in, reluctantly. "You'll be able to groove the streets, if that's what's worrying you. Just suck them good earth vibrations while it lasts. Up your left leg and out the right."

His voice wailed supersonic thru the telescope's small cannon.

It evaporates.

*   *   *

Evil Companion a primary putz pattern in Amur'ka.

United persecuted gink, geep.

Determined war not again bespoil sandlot.

Understanding noblest depth humanistic national noses.

Therefore declare:

1. Kook boss.

2. Boss Queen.

3. In sex, unity and opposites equal.

4. In Argentina, Chaim Weizman is alive and living under an assumed name

around a lantern glow on Red Mountain with dubious allies — Ira and the Breather.

"How many times you done what I just finished?"

Fat grin flashed Spoddy that the Breather always

grinned, from cackle to hearty-har-har. Trust a man constantly mile-long? "Many, many times Spoddy. And you get more spaced-out each event." Dips a hand into breast pocket of army fatigue jacket, beneath burnoose, presses coin to my fingers: "Take it man. From the Breather — your tuned in, twisted out, streetpeople brother."

It was a Chinese penny, Ming dynasty circa, with square hole in the middle

Evil Companion — YOU TAKE THE LEAD IN THE TROUGH AND THEN WONDER WHY

". . . so,"
I giggled, "am I supposed to wedge this on my belly-button and have Barbie come a-lapping mah prick?"

He smiled the weasel smile. Gesturing expansively, said: "Man, you're pathetic. When you going to learn what liberty's about?" The same hand dug into a back wheat-jean pocket and it resembled a bankbook. Shot the cover at me — *IF* — in bold lettering. Breather fondled the booklet closely. Sententiously: "I wanta read you two guys something. It's so amazing it changed my life. Dig," and rocking his shanks back and forth to discipline the earth, began . . .

" '*If* you can keep your head when all about you
    Are losing theirs and blaming it on you;
   If you can trust yourself when all men doubt you,
    But make allowance for their doubting too' "

97

and
his cosmic justice eye raked me. He was visibly moved
by Kipling's virtuous head.

   " '*If* you can wait and not be tired by waiting
      Or, being lied about, don't deal in lies' "

                                    and
elbowed me savagely in the ribs.

   " 'Or, being hated, don't give way to hating,
      And yet . . . ,' "

                        his voice dropping two notches,
Evil Companion tickling
                        "don't look too good, nor
talk too wise;" and stopping to evaluate saw me squirm,
said: "I don't want to *weary* you, Mr. Spoddy," in cold
combed voice.
   "It's not that."
   Slipping the booklet back into his pocket, red beard
drooping, goes ironic.
   "It was maybe *beneath* you?"

                        EQUINOX EMERGENCE
EVOLUTION — Evil Companion
                        and I'm bucktoothed
brokenheart.
   "Dig it," I start softly as the mouthmeter clicks,
"while you're bullshitting they're burning children to a

frizzle . . . . You're Kipling — mine's the Evil Companions, Provos, beatniks, pleiners, nozems, teddy boys, rockers, blousons noirs, hooligans, mangupi, stilyagi, students, artists, misfits, anarchists, ban the bombers . . . the last elements of rebellion left."

The Breather fiddles with the gas lantern and Ira folds his legs to lotus position. Spoddy relishes the pink glow behind his ears. Who sweats in a forest after midnight?

Get oppressive: "FUCK YOU! FUCK GRAMMAR!" The greatest poetry is the alphabet in disorder. Breather, steal a gun today . . . the 26 letter alphabet used by Europeans is *the* key to the duality of their spirit: the resurrection and the apocalypse. The first 13 letters are Christ and the 12 apostles (letters A thru M, AM, or affirmative). The second 13 are the Antichrist and the 12 antiapostles (letters N thru Z or Nazi, Nietszche, negative).

ABCDEFGHIJKLM NOPQRSTUVWXYZ

a n d
Breather, the cities will explode L-O-V-E/H-A-T-E riffs. Every variety of people weave past each other on the sidewalk. Beatniks, A-head warlocks, TPF policemen in groups of three, spades, Puerto Ricans, Inscrutable Chinese, fat Jews and oily disintegrated women doing the shop-shop routine. Side street groanings of cards and dominoes on sidewalk tables. Teenagers chop baseballs. Kids open up fire hydrants and cops chase

them away. Spanish music blares from Club Popular Members Only. Spades rock on the concrete to portable phonographs:

Everybody get on your feet,
You make me nervous when you're in your seat.
Throw off your shoes and move your feet,
We got a dance that can't be beat.
Get your high-heel sneakers on,
You know you're steppin' new.
The way you shake that thing mama,
The way you're steppin' too.
You know you're all right.
Lord you're outta sight.
Hey, our brothers have Brooklyn
Standin' up pretty nice.
Yeah, dig it.

*   *   *

Carlos moves forward in rhythmic lunges and his opponent backs into the street. Someone jumps into a car and presses the horn in an attempt to get help. Carlos' knife slides into the man's belly and he falls forward. A red net spreads across the pavement. Instantly a plain-clothesman appears and pins Carlos to the wall with his gun. Puerto Ricans encircle him as he waves his piece at them.

Get away or you're liable to get shot.

The people continue to close in.
Are you the man? Yeah, I'm the man.

He shows his badge. People scatter and wander home as if nothing has happened. Sirens close in and Carlos is taken off. Every Father's Day Carlos gets in trouble.

*   *   *

In the Tibetan Room of the Under Christ Mystery RiverRiverRiver when I asked to turn the spirits on, he said, smiling on his silver headband, they're on. Teresa, Sister Marie, Empress of Ooze beauteous bust up blameless monger of earth. From the center of the earth, the Cuban said, from the center grow the saucer flowers. The policeman bobs his head to the flattery of the priest. Goyim watching over all. Goyim shrieking to pierce the tombs of flesh. Blue gold. Goyim have planted their saucer babies and music amplifies waterfalls and purple orchids as large as two canyons. What is there left but numbers and their endless repetitions? Using numbers that exist, 36, 58, 68. Inventing new ones. Every number is a way in

CONNECTIONS ARE ENDLESS PLUM TREES — Evil Companion

and on the vicious Red Mountain your child Spoddy threaded his needle.

First address — 66 Racist Row.

101

Crowley's number — 666
Helvetius meets the philosopher's stone — 1666
New Kids learn their bodies — 1966

Suspected

jillions of gutter children got the message.

19th Nervous Breakdown: Route 66
1066 Norman Invasion of Britain
1666 Great Fire of London (destroys the Black Plague)
1916 Easter Rebellion in Ireland
1926 British General Strike
1936 Spanish Civil War (European conflict begins)
1956 Hungarian Workers Revolution, Suez Crisis,
      Freedom Rides, James Dean phenomenon
      turns us around
1966 Youth Riots, Insurrection, Anticolonial Wars
      of Liberation — World Confrontation of
      Awakened Men
1999 * * * * * * *

*   *   *

THE EVIL COMPANION A RED ROOSTER OF
SUBVERSIVE FEEDBACK

permanent youth knife :: science fiction hallucination
:: blackout power :: warlocks of the world your night
:: underdogma :: out of the void :: psychedelic guerilla
:: cosmology :: studies of forbidden knowledge ::

anarkey :: the 0th International :: mongolian invasion :: towards the new human species :: unreason :: book of the :: provotariat teenrevolt :: cultural invisibility :: trip a day :: riff jackals :: bike chains :: out of the wood-work ::

THE EVIL COMPANION WARNS THE SLAVE-CONSUMER

Well this cat they talkin about I wonder who could it be cause I know I'm the heaviest cat the heaviest cat you ever did see. When you see me walkin down the street think twice and then lets speak. On their faces they don't wear a smirk cause they know I'm the king of the cool jerk. Cool jerk cool jerk cool jerk cool jerk. Look at them guys lookin at me like I'm a fool. Deep down inside they know I'm cool. I said now I said now the moment of cool has finally come. When I'm gonna show you soma that cool jerk. Now gimme a little bit of drums by himself there. Now gimme a little bit of drums. Now gimme a little bass with those eighty eights. Ah now you're cookin baby you're smokin. Now everybody I want to hear you all.

666/666/666/666/666/666/666/666/666/666/666/666/

*　　　*　　　*

. . . . . . and the Breather stood over us, chiaroscuro princely by lantern-light, said: "I'm digging it deep veins. I'm convinced there's what there's nothing left from tomorrow except believe in YourSelf don't believe in nothing else and keep the faith rebuilding" . . . . . . and the Breather stood over us, chiaroscuro princely by lantern-light, said: "I'm digging it deep veins. I'm certain the siddis what cities the siddis what cities why prolong the agony the siddis what cities are siddis the cities . . . funky vibrations . . . still . . . ," his aura dissolved.

Dead Dualism: Spoddy, Breather, Ira, Bihder brothers, Liz the localized troll, Barbie, Joe Eppus and orphans initiated to post-'45 mutant gene Bullet Wound Quasmos.

Dying: Hitler's hangnail.

Evil Companion — EAT OF THE EYE-BALL FEAST
Evil Companion — SUPPORT THE UNIDENTIFIED
FLYING OPPOSITION, SIGN OF THE
FIRE HORSE
Evil Companion — SUPPORT THE FRATURGENCE OF
HELL'S ANGELS AND HEAVEN'S
DEVILS
Evil Companion — AFRICASIAMERICA
Evil Companion — BANISH HIPOCRISY
Evil Companion — LONG LIVE THE WORLD
REVOLUTION OF YOUTH
LET THE STATE DISINTEGRATE
LIBERATION OR DEATH

But Spoddy fell into a binary computer, a thermo-nuclear bomb, a frog pond — his skull — and almost awoke.

Almost isn't subtle.

9 / Bring Logs — Bring Fire

"I'll smother her baby."
"Initials of Freud, Einstein, & Darwin is FED."

*   *   *

Behold Ira and his carbuncular kid brother — Harold.
We shake hands, mittmasters.
I insist:

Last summer, there	CRY WHY!	"When we do good
was dancing in the streets	DEFY TO RECTIFY!	No one remembers
This summer, it's the	BREAK TO MAKE!	When we do bad
land of a THOUSAND	FIGHT TO RIGHT!	No one forgets."
dances . . .	LIVE TO GIVE!	Hells Angels
HERE IT COMES!	SING TO BRING!	Motorcycle Club
	FREE TO BE!	

Harold, a pale bedeviled youngster, replies: "Yup," taking some deepdeep breaths. "Fundamentally the Harold-scene has changed. Just before I came over here I destashed my Stuff, filled my pipe, lit my match, and AWAY WE WENT, the four of us, a suite-mate and two friends, only one of which had ever messed with Stuff before, he and I were the only ones to get high. We all had about 12 healthy

106

drags apiece, and the other kid hallucinated a polar bear and drew it, only for me to notice that its left foot was actually a masterful caricature of Meher Baba. The only bad thing about the whole thing was that I was impelled to, or more specifically, *into* my third homosexual experience. It was sort of kidding at the time, though, and I haven't felt upset about it since, so what the hell? I keep my Stuff hid in 9 Columbia Reviews stapled together with a hole gouged out in the center. All this on a school night . . . . My social life, unfortunately, is considerably less exciting than my hmm, hmm, Stuff life. I'm weak. I'm not even talking about my *fucking* life, which is quite non-existent . . . . But anyway, about a month and a half ago, on Saturday night, everyone had more or less disappeared on dates on subways or monstrous abstract-expressionist canvases stretched across Long Island Sound, and I was terribly lonely . . . when knocked on my window David Wilson, a learned pedantic intelligent bland cynical queer, good friend of mine. He immediately realized my condition and told me about a party he could get me to. Seems a friend of his, and to a lesser extent of mine, has an aunt who knows a woman whose daughter was throwing this party on Park and 91st, and this guy was supposed to bring along two kids from Columbia, Wilson and one Isaiah Spector . . . ."

IF YOU KNOW WHERE I'M AT, YOU'LL KNOW HOW TO FIND ME — Evil Companion

". . . Is this tiring you, Spoddy? Well . . . ," flowing over his chair like oatmeal pacifist when the chips are down ". . . everybody likes me better than they do Isaiah Spector, so I got dressed, told the doorman my new identity, and took the elevator upstairs. I told the hostess who I really was. She didn't know the difference, since she'd never met any of us before anyway. All,"

Evil Companion —

USE IT BEFORE YOU LOSE IT

". . . yeah, all Columbia boys fuck alike in brightly lit hallways in rich apartment houses anyway. So the four of us Mr. Spoddy — we had much to the hostess' disconcertion brought along a chick, the only girl at the party who wasn't in Dalton 1965 — the four of us sat on a couch in the living room and after our initial attempt to make contact had been rebuffed, we bitched and cut up opulence, like we said: 'We're scholarship students and proud of it.' Occasionally we'd hear preppies mutter, 'Columbia's an overrated academic institution.' And I murmured as if in a trance, 'I have to make a killing, I have to make a killing,' but nothing happened. The hostess' mother kept staggering around crocked with a huge tray of sloppy joes shrieking out 'TAKE one, you wanna get on the goo' side of the hostess, DON'chya?' I kept eating sandwiches and downed about 14 cokes . . . ,"

hesitating,

dusting off his Navy blue pea-jacket, bought from a wino on Avenue D who accepts credit cards

"... it's vital to my problem, this story. Listen: the girl's father was wearing a red dinner tuxedo and acting so servile I thought he was a hired hand, and there was an innocuous old Negro maid who went around cleaning ashtrays, and two blonde preppies who with guitar and banjo sang in ridiculously 'pop' harmony a couple of old-English ballads, and when they were done shouldered the fabulous instruments and walked off muttering to each other. Well, that's enough, except they said it in French. And Wilson and I stood on the side near some bookshelves arguing about the relative merits of Blake as opposed to the Romantic poets, and Donne as opposed to Milton. 'You want everything to be so immediate,' he kept insisting. 'You're right,' I finally said. I actually would like to continue describing this little scene to you forever Spoddy, but it does have a point, this story: while I was talking to Wilson I noticed a chick sitting by herself on the couch. Muttering under my breath 'I have to make a killing' I walked over to her and seated myself, coughed until she turned around towards me, and began with my favorite gambit: 'What's a nice girl like you doing in a place like this?' Well, she looked surprised for a moment and laughed a bit, quietly, but I didn't want her to back down, or I was too shy to say anything else, but *anyway* she had to carry the ball, as it were, so to speak. She came back, much to my disconcertion (isn't that a wonderful word), with 'What do you mean?' Oh,"

and here Harold toppled off the chair onto the shit-chute, in

Evil Companion —

ALL FALL TO FIRE, EARTH, AIR, WATER

"I was astonished and baffled, but once again it didn't seem worthwhile to back down or force or whatever for a dipshit chick at an Upper East Side thing, so I started talking talking talking about all my prejudices, ambivalences, envies, hatreds, and so on that center around money, lots of money . . . ." Evil Companion

WHICH

IS AS TRANSIENT AS WHO? — "She was

receptive.

Eventually turned out she was interested in literature, read a lot, mostly Pound and Lagerkvist — a queer couple, as Rimbaud says — and I could see her again, her name was Andy — Andrea Bluemoon, 8th and 90th. 'Any relation to the composer?' I asked jokingly, thinking of Robert Bluemoon, dead — sigh! — these hundred years, and she said 'Yes, he's my father.' Except that's Harvey Bluemoon, lousy composer, former Presi-

110

dent of Druidyard, current director of Lincoln Centaar. I was, Spoddy, sort of taken aback, but we talked about music a bit, of which she has extraordinary knowledge for obvious reasons. Turns out, also, she's a pothead. Wants to go to Radcliffe and should have no trouble getting in . . . I was great living you guys . . . ."

                                                                    stood
and paced the room, weaving a pattern that seemed to mean more and more as time went on, as time went on

(pale/intense) "*However,* it's sometimes sort of hard to establish boy-girl sexual rapport with a chick who has no environmental connection with one's self, you dig? Besides, I get a chance to see her about once every two weeks. All fucked up that way. We *talk* a lot when we're together, but only about experiences, likes dislikes, etc. We talk a lot about Stuff. I'd like very much to make her — emotionally — but she seems to know so many millions of cool people, and it takes a pretty long time even for an intelligent chick to realize just how cool I am, *I,* the master of the uncool hippies. But, anyway, the result of my meeting her was that I didn't feel all horny either sexually or Castle-of-the-Interiorishly — I feel rather like a eunuch. This frightens me a bit, but it's much less upsetting than fits of depression/despair/destruction/death, eh?"

                                                        s h u t t l e d
across the floor to the 50 lb. marble waterpipe mit the

fuzzy Turkish tubing, puffed and said:

"Should I quit
school? Should I join the jillions of kids screaming

AWAY

UNSTONED ROLLING STONE REALITY! LET THE STONES
SPEAK! LET ALL ANCIENT THINGS SPEAK! CHILDREN
CHAINED BE UNCHAINED! WITCHES ARISE! NO BARRIERS!
SPERM IS COSMIC MEDICINE! AWAY MONSTER STATE! —
Evil Companion

. . . or something along those lines, I
mean, no lines are straight in Nature . . . . Turning on
with acid would help, I guess. Pot's passé. If you can,
Spoddy, get hold of some peyote for me, O.K.? And do
you think the solution is to quit school and waste down
on E. 7th Street, get burned by Spanish Eddy, live in
ramshackle hovels of near youth shooting amphetamine
around the clock until my peripheral nervous system is
jagged, and then have drunken jigaboos weep in my
lap that they don't have enough money to go to their
mother's funeral in Alabama? Is that it? The solution,
for instance?"

*   *   *

Ira and his young embroiled brother, Harold, split
for Woodstock, New York.

Refused consolation. Kept mum. Knew our civilization would be destroyed by subtler alchemies than

nuclear war. The guilt-ridden rulers of the earth will be faced with an infinitely more personal violence of insurrections, youth riots, and the lustiest pillage since the downfall of Rome.

Psychedelics are the alchemy that will transform the mind.

Pyrotechnics are the alchemy that will transform the cities.

Spread the Word!

10 / Old People Sucking Sounds

Spoddy the goniff.
Was this Fair? Is there no worldly Justice, no Fair?
What's happened to what's Fair and Just? No Fair? No
Just? Love that tin-star permanent while hooked to
steampipes in the precinct basement, bucket of piss
wedged over brow? So the brothers said: "Bite, we bite
the titties of the Lord. Is there no Justice, no Fairlady,
fa fa fa?" The passion kids imported 500 blackmen
trumpeteers to dilute the mob. From their old air-
machines — *Bread & Liberation Special* and *A Priest
Called Handjob* — they tumble inkbottles midst
milk . . . "Them niggers got guns!"

*   *   *

Spoddy, an all-the-time goniff decided to ride a subway, walk a kitten, fly a boat, embrace with sandpaper
an ascetic genius on 13th Street — "Great is *Grrr*-eat"
— and with two southsiders and another person from
the suburbs who were passing through the neighborhood of the rioting in a car, stopped for a few minutes:
JUST LONG ENOUGH FOR THEM TO OVERTURN AND SET FIRE
TO A POLICE SQUAD CAR.

114

*　　　*　　　*

Spoddy was 'aware' of the ignorance of his actions —
as valueless as government treaties with the Indians —
which government? which Indians? As valueless as
summit conferences with the unconscious, as livid as
". . . and we will not hesitate to tear every document to
shreds, including this series, to restore the magical bal-
ance of memory and desire. Cough up your identity
and defense on these pages, a meal no man or woman
can truly digest" but this didn't amount to a penny-
whistle flying fuck in what the old people call the Long
Run.

*　　　*　　　*

The Do Right Boys come for you, sirens and flashing
lights. "Break those chains and run!"

*　　　*　　　*

A civilization rises and falls in the whorls of my palm
while smoking DMT and this nice lebanese brown hash
gifted from the Grand Street gardenia girl who neither
shortcounts nor annoints with baby-oil her booty. I
swear to Jesus in his racially permanent employment
as the Christ that my girlfriend Barbie is a woman trying to be the following at 19 years old: she likes me to
ball her cat fashion. If there are a thousand cunny ladies in a dancehall, Barbie will not be singled out. She

115

is making an embroidery of the field going God to Spirit to Energy to Substance to Life to Mind for hanging on her someday husband's wall. Red and Black wool. Her desserts are cheeses and vegetables. Floppy satin pants and gowns for her, the barb of bubbly Barbie. She thinks the Invasion begins Friday night — daylight savings time. She hopes for ten good years before the Apocalypse. She has pleasure kneeling on my belly and tongue dabbing my brain. "Your eyes, Spoddy, are bird hearts." Cheeks puff and whinny. Famous lady arm concessions. Spoddy sniffs her pits like a repeater in the joint for mashing, a spy on the all girl schoolyard.

*   *   *

When Spoddy asked her to be his wife . . .
"Children shouldn't raise children."

11 / Some Hate Capitalism

SURGENCE LYSERGENCE MERGENCE — Evil Companion

"...
death, death," shrieked Ira, his face pumping yellow-red-green Zodiacal umbrellas, thudding to spectrum paucity, "I shot the DMT yesterday and my serotonin went woundout which is known in some circles as schizophrenia. Is the world I saw real? Is my entrance into coffeepot reality . . . ? I mean, I shot DMT and felt the vultures from another world chewing. I mean, I shot DMT and like you did I thought I was dead. Y'hear me?"

Stirring afternoon tea: "I heard you. What's more, we're angry children because we're angry children. Some children ain't angry and what we got to do . . . ."

"4KU — always telling people what to do to do not." His jaws ground like an amphetamine freak churning for congress in the tropics. "Hear me out — did those electric devils give you the jitters? Forever and ever?"

Given momentum of the thousand year conflict cycle . . .

Tucked me chin in, hesitant. "Well, as it were . . . ."

Ira set another chunk of hashish on the cigarette and

sucked the smoke thru a straw. Squeaking, "Spoddy —
listen to a friend. Breather is the first real-to-karma
mystic I've ever preyed upon . . . like the old goyishe
women sucking the Christ's blood at the foot of the
cross. Jesus knew the score. He tackled the Beast

Evil
Companion — SNIFF THE STAIN ON YOUR FINGERTIPS: I'M
THE BEAST

and won. But he stopped at God. I'll create
my own gods. I'm a sleeping god. Nobody's ever inter-
preted it that way before. Christ and Buddha and the
rest of the godhead boys didn't go far enough. It's all
in Revelations to St. John. Except who's satisfied kiss-
assing One God? Like No. 666 said, it's monism-dual-
ism-nihilism and all together. Am I making sense?"

"Of course not, you're paraphrasing me." Grinny-
grin-grin.

Leaning in his chair, the hash having slumped him
to jello, whispered: "I'm a speck in the cosmic order."
Hissing last breaths, "We're all specks in the cosmos.
Nothing but specks. The War doesn't matter, because
we're specks . . . ."

News for the day. Slicing hash with a razor blade I
asked gently, "You born a Jew?"

"What of it?"

"O nothing," I replied, "except wit' me it was Catholic and I know the nun riff of withdrawal. Man, magic

118

is a much older riff, trebly potent."

He considered a moment

Evil Companion — FOCK
UP THAT CHILD'S MIND, THE BIHDERS

and Ira snatched
the remainder of my knuckle of hashish, Afghanistan
origin, drew it to his face and chewed.

"What the . . . !" and, snatching a butterknife, wedged
his horsey jaws open, as in Croatian Wedge Suffering.

He lost a tooth screaming, "Anti-social parasites!
Anti-social parasites! Is that what we are? Is that what
we are?"

A moment before the mortal flesh goes, maybe you'll
know. To 'Know' something is to 'No' it. A moment
before the mortal flesh goes. Maybe.

When?

*   *   *

'Ahoy!
Anecdotes of Atrocities,
by, with, or about Asatrucker
have begun to repel.
Seduced by his Roommate —
Engaged in Apocalyptic Preludes —
Threatened by Involuntary Psychotic
Reactions — it Appeared the RADIO
had triumphed.

119

Don't dismay:
Anecdotes of Atrocities,
by, with, or about
             Asatrucker
have compelled and renewed.
For Instance:
His Roommate, disguised as the most
Orange Prohibitionist of Krishna in
Little Newark,
Informed Asatrucker that,
truly, Asatrucker's own
Mother Oven had Tricked to the Authorities
    . . . and must . . .
according to my SHOEDOG Goor,
Be Done In.
Asatrucker,
Fearful for his Mother Oven's
                    Welfare
ran home and, bundling her in
Placemats, obscured her in the
Attic with a foam lover.
Then, covering his head with a Dust Mop,
Armed with a Sawed-Off Shotgun,
Took her place in Overheated Bed.
But!!!
Over-Confident Because Armed —
fell asleep especially early

that night.
UndercoverofDarkness
His Roommate

metamorphosed into the
foul persona of none other than the
Lachrymose Bihder! did a B&E on the
cellar window (when the fireman's
wife next door approached him with
infant-in-arms and demanded slab of
identity, he peeled off his armpit-
length black rubber gloves and said,
"I'm Albert Jones the paperman. I
come to deliver paper. I come to
pick up paper. I'm Albert Jones
the paperman. I like paper. Do you
like paper? Do you like paper? Do
you like paper?" and sent her home
multiple o'ing, something the fire-
man never tried to do) leaped up-
on the moist cellar floor, babe of
the abyss, and Crept thru the house
till he reached Asatrucker's Mother's
Overheated Bed.
(What would you think if I tried that?)
Asatrucker suspected nothing.
Shouting: "Hi! Hi! Hi! I'm 8/9/45
and I like to Bite. Hi! Hi!"

quickly tied Asatrucker up who pleaded,
"It's me, man! It's me, man!" over and
over.
Then the Lachrymose Bihder did 5000
micrograms of

L*S*D

in a yard-long spike
and injected "The Vile-Magic Mold"
into Asatrucker's cornhole.
"It's me, man! It's me, man!"
His very Words held fast.
"Don'chya recognize me? Don'chya?"
His very Words.
"OOOOOOOOOOOO I'm flippppppping . . . ."
and the Bihder:
"Bite. I like to Bite sugary worlds."
Soon, according to Asatrucker's story,
he became a "modal thycothith" replete
with ". . . worms, maggots, flying saucers,
giants, and suchlike things invade your
mind. They are out to destroy you. You
feel utterly alone. You do terrible
things — murder, for example — but only
in your mind. You perceive how small
and insignificant you are, and how enor-
mous this earth is. You see blood flow-
ing everywhere and realize it is your

fault. You lose all track of time, and
all interest in anything, except what
is happening. You can't bear light or
sound, for it is greatly magnified.
Oh, Mr. Muggeridge, no angels sing
in this place! As for instant sex —
that's really amusing. Not once while
receiving this treatment did I even
think of sex, let alone feel aroused.
I talked to my psychiatrist about this
and he told me he had never heard of
a male having a shaft under this uh
drug, yeah . . . drug . . ."

        and more distortions
familiar to Asatrucker's character.
However,
Bihder staggered the cruelty by
rapping two sharp carpet tacks thru
Asatrucker's shell-like ears.

A Pain Cycle
A Pain Cycle
A Pain Cycle
A Pain Cycle

    rang

A Pain Cycle
A Pain Cycle

A Pain Cycle
A Pain Cycle

    clang

A Pain Cycle
A Pain Cycle
A Pain Cycle

     bang

Take to It?'

Evil Companion — A PRAYER TO LUCIFER

God of light bearers, known of old,
God of the rebels, free and bold,
Sound forth thy trumpet! Let us hear!
Its silver notes ring far and clear!

In this stricken, slave-cursed world
Let now thy thunderbolts be hurled;
In freedom's name, for truth and right
God of my fathers, hurl the light!

Send out once more thy clarion call
Life to the brave! Death to the thrall!
God of the rebels, lead thine own
Behold the Bond Lord on thy throne!

Breathe on them thy mighty breath!
To mutiny stir the doomed to death

124

To revolution or their graves
God of my fathers, call his slaves!

From liberty's unconquered halls,
In freedom's name, for truth and right,
God of the rebels, hurl the light!

by Covami

IS A RIFF NOT
YET FULLY BLOWN. FAN THE FLAMES OF
a real good time
to happen quite soon. Spoddy calls this good time Revolution. I embody it. I facsimile the easy

QUABALLAH

CURB ALLAH

— Evil Companion
and the suffering entailed.

Sundown Magic Alice sparkled and pounced to the
door. She sensed Barbie shimmying in the hall. Her
cat-eyes flameth. Her tail beats the earth, pulse rhythm.

"Guess," said she, "who used to be witty and gay
before she rubbed acid in the corner of her orb and knew
misfortune. Guess who's sentenced to a life of cysts
and boils. Guess who forced her heart and nerve and
sinew to serve long after depression and held on when
there is nothing except — except — except . . . ."

Except me. Except you.

"Let's make it, Spoddy."

"Sure, baby, make to break."

And I come on like Leo the Lion of Light. An armed robbery for sport. Tear the blue fuzzy sweater from her shoulders. Take my finger-razor and split her pink down the ancient middle Way. Into bed we jump. She goes from my arms and runs to the kitchen . . . .

"The Gold-Ball Game!"

Barbie spreads seedless green grapes, four bananas, peaches, plums, watermelon slices, and kumquats on the sheets. We balled atop it. A Yin spectacular.

Sucking my blueberry hill devilishly, ". . . glad to be back, glad to be back . . . ."

My girlfriend's back.

12 / Bamboozled on Prime Time

Evil Companion — BARBIE SOUNDS BARBAROUS, BAR-
NACLES DRAGGING YOUR HULL, CRUDER THAN THE
GAMMON LUSHY IN THE SHED. AN UGLY NAME, SPODDY, IS
AN INFESTED ASS. BARBIE PUTS ON THE BARMY SHTICK
AND BALLS STALINOID KIDS WALLED UP BEHIND THEIR
FOURTH AVENUE FORTRESS. WISE UP! WISE UP! DITCH THAT
REVISIONIST PIG BEFORE SHE INVADES LITTLE NEWARK
SHOUTING 'IT'S OMINOUSLY LATE' AND 'Y'ALL GOT MID-
TERMS ON MONDAY LASTING YOUR LIFE AWAY'

"up Evil
Companion's you-know-what," said Barbie, as she laid
before me a detailed breakfast of Polish sausages, tomato juice, eggs once over lightly, and a stick of French
bread what stretched from here to Moscow and back
again with a note

CAN THE ANARCHIST TRIPE — Evil
Companion

and then she's got the gall to say, "Meta-
physical security ain't worth the fear it stands on." She
brushed her black hair, patted lanolin into her Botticelli
neck, and said: "You see, Spoddy, I love you. I love
you. And when I ask you to walk with me in dappled

sunlight — just adoring sunlight showering over you, I mean it. I want to BE with you."

Now gets reactionary again. Rebel girl asleep. Spoddy's groin foible is sparkling so she pledges allegiance. Naturally I chew my food: naturally I digest.

Dipped a fork-end of sausage into ketchup blot, glad to learn carnivorous origin. Glad to have her back. Despite her dubious habit of combing dandruff into my dessert, I dug the solace, the scissor kick. Behind her words? I comforted, "It's really good not to have to chalk up you to experience, a deaf judge. Now you're here. I'm flipped!" Pushed bread soggy in egg-yolk. Belched.

She massaged my back.

"Terrible Spoddy, O Lord." Working those thumbs counter-clockwise, "Some mothers are ruining your life. I don't mean the dope deals. It's the societal conflicts, like do-it-my-way, like taking off kids trying to score acid, in from Long Island. Stooping to Spanish Eddy's sewer?"

Again, again, again, again. I hear "against."

She gasped as she saw my crest lying in the eggs and sausage, which I'd stirred to malted-milk consistency. "You half-ass. Your crest fell down. What the fuck is wrong with you I don't know about?" She took a fork and gingerly lifted the dripping crest. In a moment it was stapled back as neat as Pocoloo's NO SMOKING.

128

"Thanks darling."

"Screw the darling. If you keep dropping that thing I'll musical-bed you for the Breather . . . . Oops, excuse the cliché."

Lodge my head in hands. 7th Street confusion. Spoddy's . . .

ARM YOURSELF AND APPEAR IN FULL FORCE — Evil Companion

and I trounced thru naive, blasé life fraction:

Kept forgetting the presidents/premiers persist. They lurk.

Kept forgetting the bankers are responsible. They hide.

"What's this?" I bellowed. "Never seen you so unfemme. What is this — some kind of Simone Whosit's kick?"

*   *   *

The Scene — A lush purple cell which constantly sort of eliminates any Jews that the occupants simultaneously wish. In stroll Adolf Hitler and Spoddy. It matters not what periods of their lives either of them are from. They are both black magicians.

Hitler: It's my turn. You act the Jews and I'll play — guess!

Spoddy: No. You played yourself yesterday . . . . Today I play the swastika nexus and you assimilate the Baal Shem Tov, melancholic Hasidic hero. Next I hurl lye in your eyes, OK?

Hitler: (fancying a D.C. plastic-puppet Prez thru a 20 yr. time slice?) No problemo. Hey, I got dis badass bopper on the line. Let's shift der whole shebang a big nort'.

Spoddy: 'Even in Magick we cannot get on without the help of others.' Remember the Man who invented you?

Hitler: 'I have seen the New Man. He is curly and cruel.'

Spoddy: No, no, the bird Thoth. (pause) Look, cool yourself out already. (pause) You know, the bird . . . Thoth. Remember how sharp his bronze beak is? Will your Tibetan mercenaries prevail?

666 COME

BIG BURDEN — Evil Companion

and she tic-tacked her hands demurely in lap. "I'm a masochist Spoddy," and her face didn't flinch forthright embarrassed.

"Pathetic warp," said I, dog-eared.

The doorbell rang. Beheld a chubby yokel who grimaced first at me, then at an envelope in his hands.

"Mr. Spoddy?"

"Tomorrow." Never in Amur'ka is the cool relaxed to strangers.

He shuffled, hillbilly messenger uniform too baggy.

"Prove it," he said. "I deliver messages to a lot of

130

people who liarize for ultimate gain. You got to prove it." This shabby man — in a limited historical sense — wanted me to prove myself. So I reached under (benches, hammock, and chairs: Indian prints and music: small alabaster lion statues sculpted by 'that demon Putney princess': a trapdoor: Sundown Magic Alice) and surfaced with passport. He stared at it. His left eyebrow jumped. "This ain't you." Wiggled his head, "Uh uh, this ain't you *nohow* . . . ."

"If that's not me . . . who is it?"

Tapping his moon on the doorstep, answered, "That's your problem. I delivered messages twenty years to congenital liars and that picture ain't you." Gliding to a new imperious vein: "Don't try to fool me!"

Called Barbie from the kitchen. She ran those wet hooks to me.

"Look at this passport photo and tell us who."

She studied it, said: "It isn't a heart-breaker, albeit evocative in a tedious sense." Her voice wobbled like wet pears in a priest's orchard. The messenger said, "See? I told you it ain't you never was you ain't go—," causing me to resurrect his 'arm?' as in Native Nazareth Shoulder Betrayal until he shouted: "Stop it! Stop! I admit guilt o-only ssstop tw-twisting . . . ." I stopped twisting and levitated the envelope from his hands — hands gnarled, mottled purple by years bearing messages to liars.

131

Within was a calling card with raised letters and embossed gold. Beneath the graphic cartoon, by way of explanation, was dashed the image of

A HORSE'S CUNT

FLAPPING IN THE BREEZE — Evil Companion

protected

by zigzag thunderbolts.

On back a note scribbled:

FOL DE RIDDLE, LOL DE RIDDLE, HI DING DO!!
YOU AND SHE INVITED TO UPSTATE CELEBRATION
ON ESTATE OF WAN CRIPPLE. FORWARD 666777
DEDICATED UNFIT FOR SERVICE ANYWHERE ON
SPECK OF CHAOS CALLED EARTH / HISTORY'S
NO MYSTERY! BLAST THE PAST! — Epira Inc.

Showed this to Barbie and asked: "Care to partake in your noxious tsktsktsk manner? Care to eradicate the Lower East Side, healthiest pollution center in Amur'ka?"

"Sounds groovy." She has black curls on nape. If we wander to the Outhouse Sanctuary, will she still be hungry? "But first you've got to shuck the whole rootytooty edifice of THE GREAT SHOEDOG OF THE NORTHERN SKY, Evil Companion, and the rest of the astral brew. I know what you're doing. But the powers you're invoking end in crystal carnage. I heard what magick does. In five years you'll be mad and penniless. Dig it," pressing her breasts to me — zestful and detached, "add up the composite of your teachers. Are they *happy*? Are they rich? Spoddy," flaunting her body like the Book of Lies, "take the familiar path to the pole of life."

She smashed my dictaphone to smithereens with a skillet. A good $200 dictaphone smashed — and I didn't even get a last void in.

"You're lovely," Spoddy says, ". . . dictaphones I got by the score. In fact I got the best dictaphone connection in town. Mr. Funny, however, is a friend. You want to see him erased too, no?"

That hit jealous home. She swept the broken machine into a corner and faced me, peasant face exasperated. Peasant face cloudy. Like flicking ashes between thighs while smoking cigs on the crapper. That cloudy, "Wise-up Spoddy! Fascist head ain't hip to our new world." She kissed me tasting chili sauce, Leapfrog Milk, boo, succotash, peppermint drops: said the silliest thing I ever did hear: "Spoddy, bare my breasts." We knew the body vortex. I unbuttoned and nuzzled her tattoo of sunburst Buddha: "You used to be an intelligent boy and now your mind is flux." Swallowed the boobs whole, knew a heatwave. "Spoddy, please please please get this — *the consciousness changes but the environment remains the same*."

Unlikely. One vibration pierces time. "Hey! a winner!" Too much

Evil Companion — TOO MUCH. ALL
TOGETHER TOO MUCH

      . . . "and how," asked Spoddy, "do
you propose to market that copout riff?"

"Market it? Never." Rummaging between my thighs
she tugged the spout to intimacy with her tunnel. Lost?
A delicate hand. Zippers and silk. But she failed me for
the thousandth time by whispering a colorful — "Imagine that low-born cowboy running amok in the Blue
Room" — causing me to snap it back and hold. She
made me

      Evil Companion — HASTY WASTY

                           flood the
dike too early.

Bamboozle on prime time.

*   *   *

Never learned to drive.

But the state 'took my license.'

I slept a shadowy house on Barbie's and Mr. Funny's
lap. Ride upstate was scenic, intersecting wooded fields
and gas stations gone sour from loneliness. A second's
doubt we'd get there carefree.

"The turnoff . . . we're here!"

It was the South Carolina Easy Box. Recuperation
takes a decade. Met at the gate by a flowing mass of
skinny hippies, I had the thing to ask: "Why — they

stretch on as far as the Eye can see." Be amusing says Ohsawa Viet Cong high in the trees laughing. These toy bandits stretch on as far as the

EYE CAN SEE —

Evil Companion

"Done with mirrors."

It was Joe Eppus in Nigerian national costume, an eleven year old boy incognito under orange / black / silver robes, beads, ringlets. He wore straw sandals. "Over your head," he confides, "is a vertigo mirror tripling all of us on the summit. Don't respect the trinity." I looked up — sure enough, a vertigo mirror. We're in the Belly of the Beast, the mouth of the hurricane. Berserk fatboy calls it 'EGO' unashamed.

"How come it isn't burning Amur'ka to shreds?"

Shaded his eyes. Pried his neck back.

"It is. It is burning us . . . . Oy! Oy!"

Mr. Funny digs kids. He likes to wrap his legs around them. Sprung from the car: "O you poorboy . . . lemme help . . . ," squatting beside Joe Eppus and cradling the child in his arms. "Easy easy baby. It'll go away soon . . . easy, easy . . . ." But Joe leaped to his feet, bopped my roommate in the nose, and ran toward a distant barn, his orange / black / silver robes streaming out behind.

"FOCKIT!!"

Ira was recidivistic. "Serves you right," he snapped.

"Nobody invited Mr. Unnatural along. Just Spoddy and his woman."

To my left: charming view of Barbie playing ring-around-the-rosie with Eppus' orphan girlfriends, on leave in the mountains. Kiss them. Stab them. I said: "Lay off. Bourgeois elements get out. Only them. Mr. Funny and Barbie are human to whose hilt."

Forgot Ira won't wear the skin of dead animals. Fur-fuck.

"So," he asks, "who digs this life form?"

Farm blanketed thousands of greenweeds. Cows nibbled meadow by silent streams. Liz the localized troll rode a greased pig in circles. Movement stirred fallen leaves. Shoes violate an inch-deep acorn crush.

Autumn seduces Red Mountain.

"DMT and nomads is what hugs me. I'll explain weekly."

By the barn door was a bold Chinese gong. Ira took a drumstick and boomed it. The door was lazily opened to this kindly brown walnut-face stuck itself thru the crack, said: "We're coming for you. Keep what you got — you're going to need it some day. You better keep what you got — because you're going to need it some day."

Heatwave made me fatmomma dizzy. Was attending a psychedelic/love/revolt orgy all the rage this hard season. 8 score people invite thousand-armed Shiva:

136

they twist and fuck for the goddess. 8 score people bind in embroidered Tantric Yoga positions, buck the jissom for aeons. This stuff is happening all over. Chiseling the girders. A good riff too. We're learning Energy Exuberant for The Struggle.

Inside the barn was a topography of 7th Street limbo. Clubs of inelegant exotics, of orphans, amused each other with corn tridents. Sweet boys discovered their lips encircled

AUM — Evil Companion

little girls likewise.

Swaying thru the flesh mist, hunched and paramount, appeared the Breather.

"You've come. I'm so glad . . . ," whipping his arms around me. "Behind that high yellow fever you were suffering in the hills that day, I sensed the faith vibrations. It makes me mighty proud to have you along this voyage." The orphan chicks turned nursery rhymes in flailed voices. These rhymes made the pricks grow. The Breather squeezed my hands between his, red mustachio tingling. Suddenly he let them drop, and his eyes screamed to cowboy size. Barbie was a mirage in the doorway.

"So . . . ."

Evil Companion won't signal. I said: "She's here — you deviationist turd. And, frankly, we don't want no trouble. She was with you, now she's under me. Please — let's not hassle over a mere pussy."

Breather thundered to the bar traffic: "Finark! Finark!" and an immense peacock's tail flutter Noah's end incense to the ceiling. Pillowed red whoosh. Spread a storm fan. Shadows raced fire in jump retreat jump. Fifteen geniis strummed zithers. Revolving red/black lamp flagged us to exhaustion. "We're Monkey Kings. Our Revolution is magick. When we touch

> FEAR IT.
> FEAR NEW MODEL EASY BOX
> GRAFTED FROM STONE ANARCHIST.
> I AM BLACKWHITE
> I AM YINYANG
> I AM PLUSMINUS
> AND I NEVER COME DOWN.
> I SEE WHAT I AM STANDING
> BETWEEN SUN AND SHADOW.
> I SEE WHAT I WILL BE STANDING
> IN DARKNESS.
> I SEE WHEN TO BE LEAVING
> (THE WILDERNESS) — Evil Companion

we devour lies. We know enemies without. Our friends are the flowers of stone."

Decided to remain a while. Lanky one long been going . . . .

"Spoddy," said the Breather, dusting seeds of Omnipotent Herb off his trousers, "I'm gonna teach you manners." Calling to his side Joe Eppus and Barbie, he draped muscular armadas around them. "I'm fussing with your wife and toying with your kid." Pecked Barbie's cheek, gave Joe Eppus a pat on the cakes, winked at me. His mouth winked. His red head winked. His red/blonde beard winked. All of the Breather

EAT

THE FISHES OF THE TREES — Evil Companion

— childhood pretender, conman mystic — foldeyed. This irked: "And Spoddy, you want to know why I do it? I do it to show you the generosity of a consciousness released from the thrall of self-interest. What's the crime of the century? The crime of the century is the death of the imagination. Me and diets and meditation and dope and deepdeep breath is reviving the invaluable factor. Dig," voice manifesting off-the-wall compassion, "I want to show you how to kiss the SHOEDOG doom goodbye."

Tunes, lights, and feather swirl receded in the fight for racial memory.

Barbed wire.

Eppus said: "Man, at Saint Boz you went berserk, a *sick* dude. Acid ain't helped you. I ain't your son. Come with me and I'll teach you nonviolent sacrifice." High forehead, lips, cute as a gopher in Nigerian national costume.

Felt airy, leaving the barn. Though my lovers insist I remain the schizoid's schizz — but divorce magick — Spoddy takes his own risks. Under State sun is continual alert. Squinting Joe led me across matted leaves. He was magnet for free legs. "Where we going, Joe? And," — affectionate shot — "why you dressed like you're making the panther, a quaint African ambush custom?"

I OWN NOTHING, BECOME EVERYTHING — Evil Companion

offers Spoddy ammo. If he speaks to sleepers of combustible lovers in China, even the hairiest look askance. If he orders his orgasms thru toolboxes, arrest is imminent. Waifs stroke my tummy for improvement.

"See that place yonder?"

Pointed to a farmhouse, green shuttered windows painted white beyond repair. Its familiarity was realized when I saw a wolfhound writhe at the end of a tether. His tail reminded me of a Little Newark smoke called Orc who had the Springfield Avenue Merchants Society in penitent relapse. He wore a white plastic deathmask to Sacred Heart Cathedral during the Christmas Eve crumbles. A cop drops his pastrami and brotherhoods: "What if we seen you dressed like that and a rape-in-progress was reported?" Scratching his conspiracy — ". . . we'd shoot you deader 'n shit." Orc plastic-bombed the stationhouse in retaliation. The blast dropped 56 officers dancing ergot-induced basement frenzy to the accompaniment of me booked for 'suspicion of coal-flake possession.' Its familiarity was realized. "Yeah . . . behind here I wrestled laughing antichrists, blew demons, initials are DMT."

We pushed by screen door

SYNCHRO-RIFFING

MOMMY IN THE BATH? — Evil Companion

and Joe yelled: "Wilbur! It's Jose and a friend, a buddy-in-plight." Living room resembled mine: remember mind? "Is this character a cripple?" I asked. Seeing people in such a condition upsets me, as in Little Newark Bisexual Blackout. "Is he? I got a migraine energy thing disrupting."

He said: "Thuggery you're quick to. Insult the same. But when it comes to the learning process . . . . How's about reaching puberty?"

"Spoddy's a child of challenge and change."

Fitting his black/orange/silver robes: "With some snow and garbage on me I'd be Pike's Peak emotion. Follow me upstairs."

Rare in Amur'ka to discover freaks who retain the old-fashioned stigmatae. Cripples' rooms, with their wave of recurrent medicine, wilted roses, have gone the way of the totalitarian nickel bag. I climbed the

141

stairs dribbling goatish apprehension.

"It's us, Wilbur. We're coming on in."

His bed was jumble of quilts. Their mince-pie geometries veered sharply at grey walls. Another wheelchair and a stool completed the furniture. His bed was punishable by death. Was intrepid. But Wilbur had many score children's books strewn about the room. "How you doing? *My* name is Spoddy." Wait for orphans to announce you and flush goeth the pride.

" 'This Body.' That's a novel name."

Hastily correct. "No no no. Not 'This Body' but," castrating carefully, ". . . the Spoddy. S-p-o-d-d-y."

"O.K. O.K." Wilbur was small boy under wraps. His head was pretty in a small goyishe way, hair flaxen, pajamas from waist up. Spoddy heard renewed sounds from the barn, as if electric winds were brooding. Whiffs of free music. Go wild go naked caressed me abrasive. Wilbur beefed: "*My* name is Wilbur Asatrucker mister. I'm looking for my dog Rickets. Will you help me find him, mister? I love my dog Rickets and want him back . . . ," beginning to weep, to whimper secret gifts.

Joe Eppus sat next to him, bed edge. "Stop the tears. Mr. Spoddy wants to meet you and," eyes glinting like Evil Companion in the shower, "*read* to you."

I said: "That's not my usual line. I'm for sin my own self."

The sick are a terrible burden. You can't whack off

142

an invalid, can't rough-house about the den, can't compare inarticulate flaw notes. The sick suck.

"Hurray! Hurrah! O read to me . . . read to me . . . !"

The sounds from the barn were louder. "Before we do that, we need quiet." So I pulled down all the room's windowshades and it sunk to a sudden hush. A peculiar phenomenon, so to speak. Turned to find Joe Eppus gone.

Evil Companion — WHERE'S A GIRL WITH LONG HAIR, EYES THAT WHISPER THRU THE HOWLING MACHINERY, BREASTS EXPLODING LIKE ANARCHIST BOMBS OF MILK, THIGHS OF CEMENT PILLARS? WHERE IS SHE?

"He's split for the barn. Tell me," tucking the quilts up to his chin, "do you think it's long before we're a full-fledged police state? Will I find my dog Rickets there? Do they draft invalids in a police state? Where's Rickets? Where's my dog, mister?"

"Cut your dog's throat, kid. Like Penrod and Sam I drown the old cur in a vat. Dig it?" The pint-size freak was bothering me.

"Mister, mister, please read to me. You came here to read to me. Read to me." So if they wanted to ditch me in the barn, why use the cripple as bait? Who but the State uses a mangled baby as bait?

Evil Companion

— THE CITY IS TENSE

and I felt, as in sift/winnow, that maybe they're Right. Evil Companion and the gangs are doing 'em in by means of the dry upheavals. Best revive limited humanism on the planet for Wilbur.

"Asatrucker . . . would your last name be Asatrucker, maybe?"

Replied in boyish frilly octaves. "Yup, yup. My full name is Wilbur Asatrucker."

Wipe my brow — give a low whistle. "Hand a book onto me kid. I'll read prose to you."

He denounced me *Miss Poodlepop In Turmoil*, outstanding youth fiction in these final years. I shoved the quilts aside and sat by this flaxen-haired invalid. Began: "'Miss Poodlepop was hoeing her garden one spring morning. She was hoeing her wild carrots. These vegetables were donated by Miss Poodlepop's niece, Petulant Penny Pushcart, a siamese cat who adored her mistress everywhere. 'Twas in the water-closet Miss Poodlepop especially appreciated her law and order . . . ,'" stopping to evaluate and reconnoiter, so to speak. Said to Wilbur — "This book is suspicious. *You're* suspicious. Where's the parents?"

I stood and tried the door. Locked. His room of grey walls, stool, books, and wheelchair also had — noticed for the first time — an oaken bucket in the corner. Wilbur whined: "Sit down and read to me please."

Scornful and told the boy: ". . . a series of incidents

in this odd room . . . they make me nervous."

He salvaged behind bangs and frail Nordic nose. "You think I'll find my dog Rickets? Know what Dis is? Dis is the innermost city of Hell. Think Rickets is at the End of it?"

Riddles keen.

"Ask the SHOEDOG. You know where the SHOEDOG is?"

But this child of ruin wasn't placated by blurbs. Next thing I'm haunting down the barrel of a .45 automatic and he's saying "Like superficial flesh wounds? O.K., where's Rickets?"

Made for the window. But he fired and the room sung orange, bitter gunpowder roar. Window pane tinkled. I wheeled around. "Alrighty now," hands above my head, "that's enough for one day."

He urged, ". . . sit down mister. I got laxatives." Handing me the revolver which I flung in a corner, he askcd, "Did Joe rat you what I look like below the waist?"

Evil Companion —

I WALK LIKE THE PANTHER

I HAVE BIG HANDS AND FEET

I SEE IN THE DARK

I AM BIT BY NO INSECT, STUNG BY NO BUG

I AM A NEW MAN, AN ALFRED E. NEW MAN

snarling:

145

"The kind of paltry spaceout who travels healed. You're a dangerous mother, I say."

Irked me to the nth power. In Amur'ka you encounter these people everywhere. Impossible to avoid. If he was at a party, he'd elbow me in the goiter and say, 'Watch the face fatboy!' I knew a character — Badfoot Bitch from Little Newark — who if he didn't get his daily truncheon ramble thru the Assyrian section it was like pedophilia. He'd come home and wake his son — 'How's about a few poundings honey?' — and beat the boy to sleep. Red welts covet my asshole.

"What's the big thing? You're a cripple, no?"

Wilbur smiled in a scary way. Then he rolled back the quilts in his lap. It wasn't an ordinary lap. I ran instantly to the oaken bucket and barfed my guts out. "Jesus Christ and Mary the Blessed Mother of God! — you're unique. That damn doughnut body is uniquer than dung."

What I meant was that below his waist was merely a doughnut of soggy flesh, half a foot thick. No thigh, ankle, or toes. Merely a loop of flesh extending from one hip to the other. Teething ring for a dinosaur.

"Please tell me your genetic makeup," Spoddy snaps.

Wilbur moistened a sponge in his saliva and cleaned his personal atrocity. "I have the lethal genes. Severe abnormalities result in death. I'll die in a straight line before the Revolution happens." Casually, he exerted

146

the muscles of his waist and lifted the doughnut three inches in the air — slapped it back down on the mattress with a phutt-phutt sound

Evil Companion —

MISFITS COME INTO THEIR OWN WHEN CONDITIONS CHANGE

. . . "yes, that's it. A town without pity . . . ."

EAT

LIMA BEANS — Evil Companion

"Think I'm a freak?"
He gave me a look of utter contempt. "I'm not interested in such things. I'm the only twelve year old boy who's got peace of mind and no legs. It took," he squeaked with grim triumph, *"thirty acid trips and a year with the Swami Boogabeeny."*

An upsetting confession. The windowshades cracked to the ceiling.

"Swami Boogabeeny? The Breather's tutor?"

"Exactly." He suddenly flipped himself to the floor. Landed with a soft phutt-phutt and — "Watch me now!" — he flipped his way toward me like an animated toilet-seat. His fragile sick face was contorted. "Swami made me au-go-go . . . ."

Repulsed by the sight, I made for the steps in a limber Latin loop, shouting over my shoulder: "Only use you got Wilbur Asatrucker is door-knocker on a giant's cottage."

"Where's my dog Rickets?"

*　　　*　　　*

"I demand an explanation."

Barbie pouted, and covered her nude with straw. Sun slanted us thru slits in the loft ceiling. Groaning.

"Apples — the only fruit I can eat and I can't get a decent apple."

"What'ya mean? These are Delicious apples."

My brethren the exotics made element changes in the oak floor. Breather's bonfire pressed black rider smoke toward the rafters where we perched. Dangerous. Ira shouted from beneath: "It's a celebration for the millions of parts that went into the workings of this enormous intestine of iron straddling thousands and thousands of miles." Meaning first-degree burns go buttery on Red Mountain.

"Did you see the apples the Breather had? Petite and hard as dog bones, the way apples should be." Below us — like scuffling beasties — violent hips burn their corduroy/suede clothes in a rash of Meat Repudiation. Watched dispassionately.

"If I can't get the kind of apples less benighted people get, what's left of our love? Why push on? Why not surrender to the Ego Police?"

Barbie rolled out of the straw and teetered on her tummy.

"Nip away the hair clinging to my ass. Spoddy, O Spoddy, I love to ball you Spoddy."

10 kilo aroma got me coughing like a Dosteyevsky consumptive.

*   *   *

Spoddy gets all bedazzled by birds-and-flowers young hippies. If he's WW2 vintage, his sisters too, they best keep an orb on the hohoho-Joes rooting for a return to the altar. Shotgun meteor panic won't merit the erection of blood gods. Take Doctor Cole for blitz instance. Didn't get his nightly operation it was like echolalia. He'd come home to his butterfly and ask: "Want a taste of the old scalpel tonight Butterfly?" And the butterfly, racked with indignation, would flutter as high as its ball and chain allowed. Black wings, speckled with red dots, eased long shadows. Each night: "Want a taste of that fine blade Butterfly?" The little darling was chained in the cellar. She got so desperately strong she managed to lift the ball and chain seven feet in the air. Fear manifested adrenaline increase. One night Doctor Cole got juiced fit to drop, stumbled down the cellar steps, and whipped a machete on the wee thing. "Butterfly! . . . I'm adopting a new foreign policy. Namely, chop you in half." Heartbreaking the way the butterfly dodged Doctor Cole's ferocious lunges. She flew so high so fast that the ball and chain assumed a

149

momentum all its own and a broad savage sweep busted Doctor Cole's head open. The iron ball did it. The good doctor is oldhat to the candyass kiddies from Long Island. Throughout the barn their exotic selves were represented. I spied Arthur Ogle: "You back so soon from that job?"

"Had to. My employer returned early."

"Really a pleasure seeing you. Barbie, say hello to the nice boy. Kiss his blue bunting."

"Forget it, fatboy."

So I said to Arthur Ogle, secretly envious of his red-eyed wealth, sublime in hyena-skin lined pea-jacket: "You spent the summer playing tennis and drinking rum?"

Arthur bounced his tennis ball off the roof cloudy with pink insence fumes. "I spent the whole summer taking care of a fag's house who went to Boston for a few weeks."

"That's living!" Slapped his back like the Serbian alderman before the voting booths of this life close. Arthur is an exception to 7th Street people. They spent the summer imitating inanimate objects like toasters and vacuum cleaners

Evil Companion — EAT CHICKPEAS

making me a pigsticking wunderkind. "I don't think I want to carnal know you twice Arthur."

"Why?"

"You've chickenshat against your kind too early."

He squashed the tennis ball into a wheat-jean pocket: "He isn't really a fag. My uncle's merely a rope fetishist. The dude told me to stay away from you I-Won't-Workers." His fine-boned aquiline face hazed. "I'm saving my ass while there's still time." Seared out the barn door, streaked toward the faint mountain refuge

GET A GRIP ON YOURSELF — Evil Companion

and my attention turned to Barbie. Thought of the suitcase days, the months roadrunning, the wooden wheels rolling thru gates of oak. For face-less reasons Barbie danced among the hippies, exhibited her cold-burning body to all who cared. Nearly everybody cared. Spoddy flung pride aside and — scattering heads in directions except South — yanked Barbie from the mob.

"The rock 'n roll is making me this way. Hear it honey."

A dozen fingers stretch out from the blonde hesitation of starvation.

The cry for bread, for life, for barricades!

Slashing music of Benny and The Dirty Face chattered me hugely and the lyrics were goody-good: find the battery/find the battery/find the battery/Don't you

lose it/Don't you lose it/or we'll run aground/
Aground?/aground/Aground? . . . . Crisp drums of
Benny doing offstage outrages. His music marks the
spot between the demilitarized zone and thou. Grabbed
Barbie by the hair.

"Have a heart. I'm gauche, but have a heart."

She enigmaed like Cheshire kitty. "Here it goes
Spoddy, here's the whole story. Listen, open the top of
your head and let it spill in. Unscrew your eyeball and
let it float free of your brain for a while. Groove my
baby on the idea of a detached eyeball, floating with a
slight spinning motion, just floating around in the clouds
ha ha ha ha ha ha ha them catching sight of . . . ."

Yanking her black/smooth/oily hair back: "Have a
heart you stoned bitch!"

Her answer was post-God pre-Nuit pragmatism.
"Find it, feel it, fuck it, forget . . . . Is that your imma-
ture thing?"

She danced away.

It was déja vu in Red Mountain barn. It was drums
and zithers, violins and Jews' harps, radio stations dele-
gating their chemical cabbage conspiracies to clap-your-
hands, dance dance dance. It was horsemen sprinting
like puppets on green carpets and sugar artillery while
the population faints from a diet of loudspeakers. Statues of heroes stand melting at attention in a rain of tears.
Giant steel roaches pull chariots with naked black girls

frozen to them. Two-headed rainbows shimmer illegal pure energy. Hippos with sea shells loaded on their backs, dwarfs herding them along with tiny daggers dipped in honey. Exotics whirl around mountains of salt. From a corner of the barn marched the Breather and Ira and a host of Others in polka-dot shirtwaists. They carried a plywood platform upon which preened a monstrous birthday cake. It was baked in olive oil, gasoline, wine, sweat, and worthless diamonds.

"Stop the music and gather." Breather took charge, arms windmilling, abrupt motions of the cosmic speck. "I got the reward. Gather round."

Circumnavigated to the front lines.

"Spoddy," says Ira, "do your friends a favor and count the candles. We need a witness."

Climbed a stepladder and begun. But Spoddy declares: "Why there must be half a million candles flaring." Polished cream, stacked in tiers, had my glands working. "I can't blow out this many candles."

Breather aimed a severe finger. "Start counting. Each flame represents a psychic/political reject. This is a celebration m'boy . . . . Count those honors."

I enumerated. "30 . . . . 67 . . . . . 91 . . . 155 . . . ," and revolved to these urban delegates, chaotic exotics assembled from the dagger thruways that throb: ". . . this is a colossal bringdown. Why do *I* have to count them?"

Ripple of applause

Evil Companion — THE CODE OF
ALL THINGS CORRUPTED

and the icing inflated. "Hey
Breather — this frosting is organic and uglier than nor-
mal." And the half-million candle jets dart near my lips.
A half-million pinhead flames lap my chinny-chin-chin.
The stepladder shook. The cake — long as a man's body
and twice as greasy — bloomed like Evil Companion's
birth. Confectionery is born upon the world. Wheelages
of hot stars pock the horizon. An anarchist dawn show-
ers up to me. Splashing blood. I don't take hands from
satin depths. Emphatically: "Eternal joy awaits you
Spoddy. Breathe!" He runs pentagrams around the lad-
der. "Breathe! Breathe! Breathe!" My face hung a
clown's cup in custard-pie sideshow. Then, candles
buckling, the cake split open.

Angry foam-flecked dog's head cavern

Evil Com-
panion — THE GREAT RUNNING SHOEDOG OF NORTHERN
IMPERIALIST SKY. RUN

and I can't budge. Can't budge
while his exciting tongue licked from bellybutton to
brow. His saliva didn't stick, as in Pathetic Canine Lap
Job. The GREAT SHOEDOG'S snout was hoary and brown.
Knobby nose. Vapours steamed from his throat in a sour
mist. What choice did Spoddy have but to kiss that bes-

tial face, grab Mr. Funny's and Barbie's hands, and trot out the barn? Was there any alternative to extradition? I dragged between them to the car.

Our mutual party brethren stamped to the safety of hills and meadows.

The ensuing blast demolished the empire of reason.

The ensuing blast left a crater ten centuries deep.

The ensuing blast made me love you.

*   *   *

Wilbur Asatrucker hunted nightcrawlers during daytime: we reconstituted in the shade of an apple orchard. Part of us did. The other kids slept it off.

*   *   *

"Barbie and I have reached an understanding. Yesterday she gave me a stereo record player, a dozen new sides."

Breather agrees in principle: "It takes three minutes for the Beatles to tell you the same as a book in a week. For what segment of your 'understanding' did she bequeath the gift?"

"The segment of me that belongs to the people."

*   *   *

In the real world's gentle airs, fever dream potential is marred by money. Without money, where's the grit?

Without the fellowship of Nod, who cares about Peking? Spoddy's not a vicious person. No! Not a vicious person. A vicious person? Spoddy never is. Without money, Spoddy is a vicious Evil Companion —

SAVORY BEEF

POT PIES CAN BE YOURS

and I found the face in the cake reprehensible.

"Listen baby," said Barbie, reading from yellow-lined letter, ". . . my parents are having a hard time selling the house. Mama says the spades are infiltrating the neighborhood, Brudder's won the Purple Heart, and Daddy can't commute no more. Little Newark is the DEATH of him and he knows it. Why's he still afraid, Spoddy? Working since the age of ten and now he goes to England for three weeks big deal," sniggering sadly. "I come home to talk of molecules and magick, they think I'm nuts. They piss on me. Daddy'll leave nothing but money at DEATH. He'll die at retirement. DEAD already. Mama has him in neurotic grip; he's got a weakheart. Mama and Grandmama hate each other alike Spoddy . . . ."

Says I: "How come you never told me you were from Newark? Thought you were an uptown chicky. Why the shame? Is the joy quotient so removed between you and them and me?"

She twiddled incandescent thumbs.

156

"I'm both, Spoddy." Revealing her phoenix tattoo hopefully, "Do you think I'm both? Love my lies?"

She jumped up, flapping scarlet chemise.

". . . tired, I'm tired . . ."

She was into her own thing: ". . . they don't know laughter, my focking parents. They laugh at old stuff. Father's a Spanish Civil War buff and washes himself twenty times a day. Mama won't eat lemon meringue, won't allow it on the same block. A year ago she slapped a Jewish lady whose meringue aroma floated across the backyard. Behind our house is a famous clothing store owner. His two sons sit on our garage roof and shoot B.B. guns at Mama hanging panties on the line . . . ," wringing the yellow letter in wash-cloth palms. "I know it's too late but contact must be made! They've got to understand their daughter somehow."

Arms around her. Blinked my eyes. Couldn't dare explain that parental contact is reciprocal or nil. If your parents are straight, forget it. Most sleep forever.

"Add to it, Spoddy, the rising tide of food prices and it appears I've tolerated your bullying too long. Out of love? Out of pity? I'm sixteen next week."

I pounced from the hammock enraged. "What!? That's the cruelest thing in the world was just uttered . . . *pity* me . . . you pity *me? Me!* — the White Lion?"

She took a whiskbroom and, tiptoe in chemise, dusted my throat. Remembered my oral lusts. Imagine the tear-

157

drops boiling my eyes like potatoes. "Spoddy," in morning peace, "I didn't mean it. I said it to scare you."

"Scare me?"

*   *   *

Why would anyone want to scare me?

13 / Themes From a Policeman's Ball

Spoddy's life is disposable mandates.

Do you believe his military horrors? So many riff them these interim evenings.

Do you appreciate his noisy defense? So few sense the need.

He rarely left his dusty house, but the transgressions of chieftains on earth absorb him. Rocking in the hammock, fomenting an Evil Companion agenda, when Harold dropped by:

"Hi there Spoddy," said the indoor involuted youngster. "There's been a change . . . I've quit Columbia and am having a portable gas. Wow!" He paced the room, clicking his fingers and loving. "Let's get high my friend."

Were conflicts churning. I stifled badness and handed him a joint. Admittedly: his eyes were hopeful, brown, jejune. Whose weren't?

He swung his legs from the hammock, looked about him. "Your house, Spoddy, is weird. Keep getting the feeling I'm in a kinda cage. I mean, that's an *easy* image — but still . . . ."

His brother had taught me the cliché of foot-long

joints. I took off and passed it to him. Greedy hands.
He looked at me, then said slowly: "Recall I told you
I'm off pot because of paranoia? Well, on Saturday night
I got depressed with the 7th Street misery and Ira was
there and we lit it up already, lit the fucking pipe already etc. — as he would say. (I'm getting blasted right
now, dammit.) And Sunday night I got very upset about
my gutlessness, my nervousness, my inability to con-
centrate, so for the past few days I've been going back
to the counseling services at the University. The fellow
did not help me as much as I thought he would the first
time, and I was quite disappointed, but what the
fuck . . ."

       rolling off the hammock and laughing when
it was least appropriate, the certain way to spot a head
in the zoo

       ". . . and thank God I got you, Spoddy, a fel-
low with a grip on himself, though somewhat schizzy
I've been told. It helps to be able to have someone to
talk to if you ain't so hot at scribblin' it down on a
fuggin piece of paper like you was some kind O' fag,
fer Chrissake. Course, I ain't insinuatin' nothin' 'bout
you, course not . . ."

       and I fed his lungs

       ". . . I mean,
after all, you's an intelligent guy, tho a dropout of the
tekno-feudal society, 'n don't fall for none o' this kind

160

O' shit, you COCKSUCKER ! ! I mean I'm sorry, kid, that just sort of slipped out, I didn't mean it, you know I have the highest regard for you, you ASS EATING PRICK ! ! Oops, there I go again, too bad, you MOTHER JUMPING FUCKFACE ! ! Ha ha, nasty tongue I have, I can't control it, you GOB OF SHIT ! ! O, I'm sorry, you PIMPLE CHEWER ! ! I mean, you FART NOSED ELBOW-HEAD ! ! Oops, you CASTRATED BABOON ! ! Errr, you MORONIC PUSSEYED PERVERTED SPINESUCKING ASSHOLE LICKING VOMIT EATING . . . why you DIRTY HORRID SMELLY EATER OF THE TURDS FROM DEAD GOATS' FINGER-NAILS ! ! ! ! !"

and Harold subsided to a squeaky wheeze. Perched on a bench, wildly giggling. "O, I'm so messed up. Ha ha ha ha, I'm a mess," burying his face in hands and sobbing.

I was careful. Needed was a ploy to stop tears. Holy ponies stampede from the north, their hooves chipping his heart.

"Dig it, Harold. There's a new saying going around: Yankee Go Home to Europe. I've decided not to leave Amur'ka after all. Instead, I'll make the classical trek to San Francisco with Barbie and Mr. Funny and others. Want to come?"

He looked up at me, face wet. "Travel with you? Man, I'll be ready to travel with you when by sheer will I go out and throw a few bombs at the NYC Traffic Com-

missioner and slit my mom's cunt up to her eyeballs —
then, maybe."

My man has a dependence problem. Who doesn't?

Spoddy loathes dialogue, personal punchouts, and
the guise of secret integers.

"I talk," he said, "without talking about myself because I'm infinitely repressed, O.K.? You're baiting me.
These hostile attacks on my constitutional reserve. True,
true, your legendary viciousness. But you don't understand me. I have no desires. Goals I've got, as academic
as before. But I don't want to get laid. I don't want
friends — except for Ira and you and your useless
crowd. I don't want a summer job. I don't want to go to
sleep. I don't want to stay awake. Dig it,"

his eyes were
gravy-brown sockets, sucking in like whirlpools

". . .
I desire only to drift along on the polluted dull currents
of my own half-assedly intellectual personality." Mum-
bling, "This is all defense mechanism."

It's a choice. The city is tense and crouching as its
insect million approach their prescribed destiny of loneliness: loudspeakers blare out the swill of the news: the
syndicated progress of district seven is nearing the limits
of the first cycle. You must choose between Evil Companion and the Sorry Kid. It's the choice of your life.

Harold began crying again, and Spoddy hated the

bastard's style.

I popped back in the hammock again, keeping one ear on the sound of Barbie dressing in the bedroom, the other on shaken Harold. I reached into

his mouth

"before leaving school I met a kid from a hip school in Boston. The thing that interests me most about kids from hip schools is that they are more courteous in the purely middle class, and upper class I suppose, ways than anyone else. They know all the gimmicks about how to puff on your mu'fu'n cig so that it looks cool, or how to light matches

E v i l

Companion — LIGHT MATCHES!

without taking them out of the match book. It's sort of faintly irritating, because — as Andy would say in an apocryphal Pound quote — why should one lie about such matters? — it is sort of admirable in a man-they-dig-the-proletariat kind of way. You see,"

becoming didactic to the boy who knows kasha knish

"there's something fatally attractive for people like you and me in this whole maze concession of motorcycles and cowboy boots and faded dungarees with thick genooine leather belts and cashmere sweaters open at the neck without tee shirts. It's a more subtle and sophisticated form of playing blues guitar, which . . ." skinning his soul

"I also do, fairly well at that. You'll have to hear me sometime."

Barbie heard that. She came into the living room carrying a towel. Her breasts quiver ivory spears. "What's this? Harold's crying." He was hunched on a bench corner, gurgling guttural grunts.

"Whatsamatter?" she queried. "Got the limp organ?"

Spoddy snuck up from behind and trapped my girl in a full-nelson: like a chick named Jo from Little Newark, cherry snapped by me before the thirteenth birthday. She had a black afghan hound. It bent obscurely its back legs when she walked it, urinating womanish doggy gesture. The afghan pissed and Jo was eclipsed to the lowest echelon of Little Newark despair — a girl hitch-hiking at four a.m. with a Bible on Route 22. I pressed tenderly the nape of her neck, said: "Don't be mean to the kid. Don't be sounding him when he's down."

She bit my elbow. "Lemme go . . . you're hurting!"

Naive, pale, fluid Harold didn't comprehend the pain rotation Barbie and I maintained. He decided to join her — foisting an alliance between Joe Worker and Colored Jim: "Spoddy, why not lay off the brutality? You don't have to impress me. What man with a Cosmic World View breaks his girl's neck?"

164

So I flare the blood and beat the shit out of Harold. His mouth bled open, fly-catching.

As I beat the shit out of Harold fury swells within as I contemplate his comic-book body. I bash him senseless. I hammer out of him all the grime eating me that morning, all the East Side horseshit. A Bisexual/ Asexual teaching.

He crawled toward the door, as I'd seen Lieutenant Pocoloo do. Almost there, when a mournful look hippie wedged his head in, a cat I used to deal with, said plaintively: "Man, this is the best smelling place, I mean like the odor of the crypt is here, and do you have any more?"

"No," I said, angry at leaving open the door to my Fuse House.

"I mean like you don't want to share it or you really don't have any more?" not yet divining that we were our own ploy and he crabgrass.

"No," I said. But he entered, tripped over Harold, and wandered from one end of the room to the other, winking at Barbie and whistling, but for him there were no hospitable benches, hammock, or chairs, and so one more, "You sure? I mean you really don't . . . I mean . . . ?" and one more "No," and he dragged out. While Barbie and I sang frantically "O so good to put in your tummy etc." the door opened again and another sharpshooter 7th Street dude with sideburns and gold-rimmed spectacles and a jaded/innocent jewbagel face walked in, asked: "Does the Evil Companion prosper here or something?"

Was my dealer's trademark. "He's retired." Which I instantly did. Not for ethical reasons. Dope is a continual kinkertop in the proper quarters. My head ain't in quarters.

Harold tried to crawl thru the sharpshooter's legs. But the sharpshooter stood heavy on left thumb. "Whoa there . . . whoa, fella . . . ."

"Leave him be," sniggered Spoddy. "He's a poor man living on a rich mommy's dole."

14 / Where It Persists

I line 'em up on the shelf. Barbie, Breather, Bihders, Lieutenant Pocoloo, etc. They're just cartoons. Evil Companion is crap. So's the Sorry Kid. Why perpetuate their agony?

I'll go for a walk instead.

*   *   *

Planet earth surrendered yesterday as the final ultimatum was delivered to shrinking humanity: go and seek your distant ways. I will find you out and make you into What You Are.

newsbulletin hallucinated in manhattan

The city of man.
The city is the hive, the big center of all-important activity, of energies and motions and an intricacy of forms and shapes, developed on itself like cement fungi. At first Spoddy thinks wow and then I perceive the creatures that inhabit the city. The city is temple, tomb, the iron and stone spoor of civilized man.
See the city. Hear the city.
The city coughs

"This sounds sick . . . but before I go I got to tell you my first acid trip. It was amazing. We listened to Bach B minor mass and D minor piano concerto *in* the RADIO and man! ! it was magnificent! And I kept closing my eyes and seeing those amazing patters and Ira did the Bihder skit to me and I was so fucking terrified it was amazing. And Ira came out with this beautiful psychodrama like this: you know this is fantastic, but I was thinking that if I had to live my whole life like this I'd go mad. And they'd lock me up and strap me down on a bed with nothing but a pad of yellow paper and a pencil and day after day I'd sit there and write 'kill me . . . kill me.' And the Daily News would eventually come around on the hospital beat looking for repentant LSD heads and the next day the headlines would scream 648 days of kill me's from Ira Fish the rotten jewboy communist acid-addict, we'll be only too happy to kill him, the skum of the earth, and Walter Kronkite would show it on his tv show: Ladies and gentlemen we are at the Fish-head's bedside in Cold Vibration Memorial Hospital, yes, he's picking up his pencil, there goes, folks . . . a K ! ! ! He's going to do it! (meanwhile on channel 4) you take it Chet. Chet: he's written the k, now comes the i, and he's gasping out the first l, why don't you take it back to main central station whoopee headquarters, David, and check on our great big presidential computer what

the odds are in favor of his coming out with the next
l . . . uh, uh, he's beaten you to it, now the m, AND NOW
THE E ! ! ANOTHER KILL ME ! ! ! ! THE SCENE IS GRO-
TESQUE ! ! PANDEMONIUM ! ! SIMULTANEITY ! !"

This is
the city: men and machinery thrown like dice on the
plain.

It was a bland barbershop. One Puerto Rican barber,
a bronze-plated horse's head, nine Police Gazettes, and
four of them chairs what rise. It was a basement barbershop.

"O.K., don't fly out of your seat. I've come for the
Nazi cut, real close." I said this to mollify the barber's
grimace. My kind of freak doesn't frequent these services on the up and up. The barber clambered out of
his chair against the wall. A strange grin twined across
his dark, gypsy-like face. I was dealing with a spic 7th
Streeter in his stuffy paradise.

He shook my five maidens. "Well howdy-doo doo
doo."

Dropped into the chair nearest the street. "Shave it
real close. I'm doing the expatriate bit next week."
Border guards and the Royal Canadian Mounties were
instructed to prevent non-militaristic outlaws from
crossing into Toronto, to inquire the source of coin-
age . . . : "Where are your monies, sir? Did you come
to Canada without monies? Ah," sighing a green whis-

key sigh, "maybe you'd best return to Little Newark, Amur'ka for monies, sir." And the absence of serial numbers. Told the barber: "Shave it close to my head. Deprive me of my Renaissance locks." He tossed a sheet over me, bound my neck in a paper collar. As he whipped a lather, asked in perfect English: "Leaving so soon Mr. Spoddy? How come you didn't write us for a Permit to Depart?"

Squeezed my eyes tightly, focusing inward orbs to spy the black/yellow glow. "I'll just make believe I didn't hear that." Hoisting an eyelid, I saw the barber still creaming lather, cutty-eyed distant from me about three feet. Tried to sit erect, but he'd cleverly strapped me to the chair.

"Lieutenant Pocoloo! Help! O help somebody!"

He ripped off his disguise, jerked my chin back in the crook of a white arm, and doodled my throat with the razor.

"Shhh . . . ," voice tapering off like snow.

I quieted.

His barber clippers sheared hollows of dirty curls fluttering my neck. He reminded me of an absorbed Italian butcher in Little Newark, the wop who caught the car thieves. Four greaser kids, hot with Thunderbird Wine, had robbed Doctor Cole's car. If they didn't get their daily joy ride, it was like a stint in the library. They drove crazily thru Little Newark streets, hollering like galoots, plowing into a front porch, smashing to tinder the legs of Vincent Marcantonio returning from catechism lessons at the Sacred Heart School For Imps. Engaged in spicy sausage stuffing, the Italian butcher saw the tragedy — "Madone, a community outrage!" — and trapped the runaway driver in an alley. "Don't do it Mister Pizzi! Don't chop it off ! !" — but the butcher grinned and severed the delinquent's lob. Said to Pocoloo: "Your imitation of spics is marvelous. None of that gargle-babble-stutter associated with foreigners." Explanation: ". . . as it were, so to speak . . . ."

He revolved the chair so it faced the wall mirror. I reflected fifteen times in fifteen barber chairs, lapsing portraits to eternity. The lieutenant mirrored once.

Struggled to get out of the chair, tried to slide beneath the belts. He watched. "Cut that out. I'll cut you free when I'm ready." Sprayed talcum on my neck. Spoddy saw cuffs and shoes thru the basement ground-level window, stockings and heels, trim ankles of prey. "Not in school, not in the army, not working — not yet in prison. What are you going to do for the next ten years? Drift?"

To distract the knife, twinkling over my throat like a flying fish, said: "Wrong. You're wrong because I applied to the Teamster's Union as a trucker. The union will train m—."

Tapping the razor on my nostrils: "Why lie? I'm talking for your own good." Rinsing the rest of the disguise off, he mocked: "You're predictable. I predicted you'd shorten yourself before Canada and pacified this shop."

The barbershop air smelled like the farts of Sundown Magic Alice, now given away. Reek of tamales, scalp bundles swept into corner pyramids. Senseless to resist any longer. Who burns a bridge of iron and steel? Who forfeits a life of he knew what he wanted? Who zips a firepole and comes out in China?

"Kill me. Go on please. Kill me dead O'Brien duplicate."

"Who . . . ?"

The lieutenant had other plans, shuddery harvest of degeneracy.

"Want to know how you permeated me that time. Try it again . . . please . . . ."

"Never."

Couldn't if Spoddy tried. Hadn't given lately. Impotent without women.

"Alright, Spoddy, it's our turn. First you're going on an indoor buggy ride," and, bracing himself with both feet, spun the chair mightily. Centripetal force tugged my eyes to a muscle tantrum. Bulging red eggs. And my backbone nearly snapped. I cried: ". . . . . hhhhhhhhhhey . . . ."

The chair rattled to a stop.

"Grasp that?" asked Lieutenant Pocoloo.

Panting revenge, answered: "Gr-grasp what?"

"Grasp the *sad*. Did you grasp the *sad*?"

Managed to free right hand and reach bone-handled switchblade in pocket. Released safety-catch, beckoned his throat within slash/sexless iniquity, repeated gambit: "Grasp what? Grasp what sad you mean?"

He roared it. "SADISTS ARE ALWAYS SAD ! ! !"

. . . . falling human riff . . .

15 / No Safety

What is more unpleasant than being pushed into fear
as the aftermath of a haircut?

My deceit maybe? My hate?

Evil Companion —
MY WANTING LIFE MAYBE? MY WAR?

or my cysts
many? My cysts?

Evil Companion — MY KILL MAYBE?
MY RED RIPPLES?

and, clicking Spoddy's frozen teeth
from skin church, I resumed membership in those colo-
nies of the restless, violent, unemployable, and raging.

Crooked on and off in menial tasks.

Designated by the State as a player, one bordering in
the dangerous state of insanity.

Sentenced to death.

Known as egolip.

*   *   *

Future with

Evil Companion — SHOULDERS BACK
AND COCK OUT!

Statement

Bad self it can get the best of you: so that's this book if weak if hardass if you're coughing up saliva in a tiny flat with undulating linoleum. You and me and we all ran together in the RYhMe gang, remember, me and Elliot tracking Barf Baby Beesley round the East Side to score skag and taking off barkeeps for their pride, pushers for poison, sure I packed a forty-five pistol, my nose was wet and runny. Was this just a runny-nosed punk? Sure. And after the mailboxes got blown (or so it was rumored) young Walter got a shank in the top of his head and died. This pale man was fine with math and curled up on the kitchen floor on acid like a cat circle curl and murmured 0 0 0 0 0 zero zero zero. Now he's murdered. Spade John shipped out. Gary's wife sucks tv and he's still hooked. Their baby battles the kitten for food. Israel is roaming and Jon's still preaching ANARKEY and does work with a homemade tarot deck fashioned from maoist coloring books. We don't see each other. Guesswho hitch-hiked round the world and met his kid brother in Kabul, Afghanistan riding hash configurations, a different bag . . . .

Bad self can be assuaged. There *is* a Path.

Bad self is what this book is about. Larry and Burk and Ward and Ben and Jon and Monk and the girls Dida, Diane, Dotty, Sybil and the laughters *wrote* it, the words, and I was the grid for their illusions. Thank you. That's the gratitude, the tears. But changes keep us dancing.

Love has so many possibilities.